**He lowered his head, bur... ...ce
against the co... ...k.
"Do you know... ...to
do this?" h...**

The breath caught in her throat when he stood up
and unbuttoned his shirt and kicked off his shoes.
Denise wanted to look away but couldn't when he
unbuckled his belt and tossed it on a chair next to the
bed. His slacks and briefs joined the belt, and with
wide eyes, she stared at the muscles in his back and
firm buttocks. She gasped again, this time when he
turned to face her.

Denise had lost count of the number of times she'd
viewed Rhett's nude body, but seeing it again made
her aware of how beautifully proportioned it was.
Years had added muscle and bulk to his lean frame. A
smile parted her lips when he leaned over and kissed
the end of her nose.

Rhett reached for the hem of her top, pulling it up
and over her head. "Are you all right with this?"
Denise closed her eyes, nodded. "Do you trust me
not to do anything you don't want me to do?"

She opened her eyes. "Yes, Rhett, I trust you."

**Books by Rochelle Alers**

Kimani Romance

*Bittersweet Love*
*Sweet Deception*
*Sweet Dreams*
*Twice the Temptation*

---

## *ROCHELLE ALERS*

has been hailed by readers and booksellers alike as one of today's most prolific and popular African-American authors of romance and women's fiction.

With more than fifty titles and nearly two million copies of her novels in print, Ms. Alers is a regular on the Waldenbooks, Borders and *Essence* bestseller lists, is regularly chosen by Black Expressions Book Club and has been the recipient of numerous awards, including a Gold Pen Award, an Emma Award, a Vivian Stephens Award for Excellence in Romance Writing, an *RT Book Reviews* Career Achievement Award and a Zora Neale Hurston Literary Award.

She is a member of the Iota Theta Zeta chapter of Zeta Phi Beta Sorority, Inc., and her interests include gourmet cooking and traveling. She has traveled to Europe and countries in North, South and Central America. Her future travel plans include visits to Hong Kong and New Zealand. Ms. Alers is also accomplished in knitting, crocheting and needlepoint. She is currently taking instruction in the art of hand quilting.

Oliver, a toy Yorkshire terrier, has become the newest addition to her family. When he's not barking at passing school buses, the tiny dog can be found sleeping on her lap while she spends hours in front of the computer.

A full-time writer, Ms. Alers lives in a charming hamlet on Long Island.

*Twice*
*the*
*Temptation*

# ROCHELLE
# ALERS

KIMANI™
ROMANCE

A time to love, and a time to hate;
a time of war, and a time of peace.

—*Ecclesiastes* 3:8

 KIMANI PRESS™

Recycling programs
for this product may
not exist in your area.

ISBN-13: 978-0-373-86180-4

TWICE THE TEMPTATION

Copyright © 2010 by Rochelle Alers

www.kimanipress.com

Printed in U.S.A.

Dear Reader,

They're back....

It's time for another Eaton family reunion, and this time it's Denise Eaton who takes center stage.

Denise, the executive director of a D.C.-based childcare center, is offered a second chance at love with the man to whom she'd once pledged her future.

However, she is unaware of Rhett Fennell's plan to seduce her and then walk out on her as she had done to him years ago. Even the best plans can backfire, and Rhett is forced to abandon his sweet revenge once he realizes he has never stopped loving Denise. *Twice the Temptation* is twice the love and twice the passion as another Eaton finds a love that promises forever.

Look for sexy ex-military officer Xavier Eaton in 2011, as he romances a beautiful chocolatier in the first of a two-book wedding series set in South Carolina's low country.

In the second book Dr. Mia Eaton will discover that she doesn't have to sacrifice her medical career for a chance at love when she encounters a hunky lawman in West Virginia's mining region.

Don't forget to check out my new Web site at www.rochellealers.org.

Yours in romance,

Rochelle Alers

# Chapter 1

"Denise? Oh, I didn't realize you were on the phone."

Denise Eaton's head popped up and she waved away the woman who'd come into her office. She couldn't talk to the social worker, because if she didn't resolve what had become a dilemma there would be nothing to discuss.

"Are you certain I have no recourse, Myles?" she asked, continuing with her telephone conversation.

After she'd opened the certified letter, reading it not once but twice, she'd called her cousin, Myles Eaton, who taught constitutional law at Duquesne University School of Law, before she'd faxed the letter.

"I'm sorry, Denise. I wish I could give you more encouraging news, but the new owner *can* legally raise the rent. You approved the clause in your original lease that allows him to do it."

"He had to have known he was going to sell the building when I signed the lease. What I can't understand is why the new owner wants to double the rent. He has to be aware of prevailing rents for this neighborhood."

Denise had chosen the less-than-desirable D.C. neighborhood because the working parents who lived there needed the services she offered, and the rent for the building where she'd set up her business was one she could afford.

"Maybe he knows something you don't, Necie."

"Like what, Myles?"

"Perhaps the area is targeted for gentrification and he wants you to vacate so he can use the property for something other than a child care center. Do you know anyone in D.C. who can advocate on your behalf?"

She rubbed her forehead with her fingers as she felt the beginnings of a tension headache. "Like who?"

"Like someone with political connections."

Denise did know someone, but there was no way she wanted to be beholden to Trey Chambers. "No," she lied.

"If you were my client, I'd recommend you contact the owner and see if you can negotiate a deal that would be reasonable for both parties."

"What's reasonable is I can't afford even a hundred-dollar increase in rent. I'm barely breaking even."

"Call the new owner of the property, Denise, and if you're unable to talk to him, then call me back. I'll look up some of my old law school buddies who practice in the District and see if they'll represent you."

"How am I going to pay them, Myles?" She only had three months of budgeted funds for New Visions Childcare and less than a thousand dollars available for legal expenses.

"Don't worry about paying them. I'll cover the fees."

Denise panicked. There was no way she was going to let her cousin subsidize her business. She hadn't accepted any monetary support from her father and mother, deciding instead to take out a business loan to set up the progressive child care center in a D.C. neighborhood where poor and working-classes families desperately needed the services.

Her delicate jaw hardened when she clenched her teeth. "No, you won't."

"Stop being so mulehead, Necie."

"Thank you, cuz. I'll call and let you know how everything turns out."

"Necie, don't…"

Denise cut off whatever Myles was going to say when she hung up. She wasn't completely destitute. Instead of subletting or renting the one-bedroom Philadelphia co-op her cousin had given her when she moved out after marrying celebrated playwright Preston Tucker, Denise had decided to sell it. After several deals had fallen through, she was finally set to close on the property. But that was three weeks away.

She had to decide whether she wanted to invest the money in the business. The profit she stood to make was enough to cover salaries, utilities, rent and other essentials for operating the child care center. The first year, New Visions had made a modest profit, but this year it was projected to increase by ten percent.

Drumming her fingers on the top of the desk, Denise stared at the framed prints of children from around the world in their native dress. She'd fulfilled a childhood dream of becoming a teacher, but hadn't stopped there. Setting up the child care center was the second stage of her plan and the third and final component was to eventually establish a school for at-risk, underprivileged boys.

However, everything she'd sacrificed and worked so hard for was about to implode. The new owner of the property had given her ninety days to accept the terms of the rental renewal agreement or vacate the property. And there was no way she could find another building, renovate it and secure the necessary permits to run a similar facility in three months.

She stared at the letter for a full minute. Reaching for the telephone, she picked up the receiver and dialed the number on the company's masthead. "Capital Management. How may I direct your call?" asked the woman who'd answered the telephone.

Denise sat up straighter. "May I please speak to Ms. Henderson."

"Who's calling?"

"Denise Eaton, executive director of New Visions Childcare. I received a certified letter this morning signed by Ms. Henderson. I'm calling to set up an appointment to meet with her to discuss the terms of the renewal lease agreement."

"Please hold on, Ms. Eaton. I'll see if Ms. Henderson is available."

Denise continued drumming her fingers, her heart beating rapidly against her ribs, while mumbling a silent prayer that she would be able to appeal to Camilla Henderson's maternal instincts—that was if the woman had any.

"Camilla Henderson," she said in a strong, no-nonsense, businesslike tone. "How may I help you, Ms. Eaton?"

"I'd like to set up an appointment to meet with you to discuss—"

"The letter you received outlining the terms of the rent increase," she said, interrupting Denise.

"How did you know?"

"I'm not clairvoyant, Ms. Eaton." There was a hint of laughter in her voice. "It's just that I've been fielding calls about rent increases all morning." The sound of turning pages came through the earpiece. "Are you available this coming Friday?"

Denise checked her planner. She had a staff meeting at ten. "What time on Friday?"

"I have an opening for Friday morning and another one for late afternoon."

"I'd prefer late afternoon."

"My assistant will call you Friday morning to set up a time and place where we'll meet."

"We won't meet at your office?" Denise asked.

"No, Ms. Eaton. We're currently renovating our offices and conference room."

"Okay. I'll wait for the call. And, thank you, Ms. Henderson."

"I'll see you Friday, Ms. Eaton."

Denise hung up. Camilla Henderson seemed friendly enough on the phone, so now it was up to her to try to convince the woman to lower the rent for the sake of the children, their parents and the employees of the center.

Camilla Henderson exhaled a breath when she dialed Garrett Fennell's extension. It took less than a minute for his executive assistant to transfer her to the CEO of Capital Management Properties.

"Rhett, Ms. Eaton called. I told her I'm willing to meet with her Friday afternoon."

"Call her back and tell her you're available tonight."

"What if she's not available?"

"If I know Denise Amaris Eaton as well as I believe I do, she *will* make herself available. Tell her to meet you in the lobby of my hotel at seven. That should give her enough time to close the center and make it to the Hay-Adams in time for dinner."

Denise parked her car six blocks from the Hay-Adams. She'd been surprised when Camilla Henderson's assistant called soon after they'd hung up to schedule a dinner meeting at the hotel across the street from the White House for seven that evening. Her plan to wash several loads of laundry was scrapped when she'd left the center at four—two hours earlier than her normal quitting time. She'd gone home to shower and change into something more appropriate for a dinner meeting at the landmark hotel that was a popular choice for policy-making meetings among Washingtonian politicos.

She didn't have time to wash and blow out her hair, so Denise brushed it off her face, pinning it into a loose chignon on the nape of her neck. It had taken three changes before she'd decided on a sleeveless ice-blue linen dress with a squared neckline edged in black. The narrow black belt around her waist matched four-inch pumps and the bolero jacket. She wore pearl studs in her pierced ears, a matching strand around her neck and a gold watch that had been her father's gift to her when she'd earned a graduate degree in educational administration. The outfit was perfect for the warm spring weather.

It felt good wearing the heels, only because her work attire was relegated to slacks, blouses and sensible walking shoes. It was only on rare occasions that she wore a suit or dress to work. The exception was when she had a meeting outside the center. Although she didn't interact as closely with the children as she had when she was a classroom teacher, coming into contact with sticky fingers or when she picked up a toddler who'd had an accident, Denise had learned to dress for practicality.

"Good evening, miss."

Smiling, she nodded to the well-dressed young man. "Good evening." Although she hadn't turned around, Denise could feel the heat of his gaze on her back when he passed on her right.

"You look very nice," he said.

"Thank you."

Her smile was still in place when she crossed H Street, heading for Sixteenth. His unexpected compliment was an ego-booster. Not only did she need to pump up her ego, but she also needed an additional shot of confidence, and Denise wasn't about to rule out a minor miracle.

She had never been one who'd found herself at a loss for words. In fact her mother had always said she should've been the model for Chatty Cathy. Paulette Eaton claimed her daughter spoke in full sentences before she'd celebrated her second birthday. Her father, Boaz Eaton, said children who were talkative were usually very intelligent. Coming from Boaz, who'd stressed education above all else, it had become the ultimate compliment.

Denise detected a smell in the air that she'd come to associate with Virginia and the Capitol district. Maybe it was chicory or another plant indigenous to the region.

Once she'd contemplated moving from Philadelphia to
D.C., she'd met with a real estate agent several times a
month to look at vacant properties for her business, and
when she'd found the one-story brick building she'd been
relieved it hadn't required major renovations. Finding
an apartment proved a lot easier for her. She was finally
settling into a one-bedroom apartment at the Winston
House. It had taken her a year to finalize her move from
the City of Brotherly Love to the nation's capital.

The walk was what Denise needed to compose herself
when she nodded to the doorman, who'd opened the
door to the entrance to the Hay-Adams. "Thank you."

Touching the shiny brim of the hat, the man bowed
as if she were royalty. "You're welcome, miss."

She entered the opulent lobby of the building that had
been originally designed in the 1920s as a residential
hotel. However, Denise felt as if she'd walked into a
private mansion on Lafayette Square that featured suites
with views of Lafayette Park and the White House.

Her eyes swept around the lobby, searching for a
woman wearing a tan pantsuit with a white blouse. She
checked her watch. It was six forty-five, fifteen minutes
earlier than their appointed time. Walking over to a
plush armchair, she sat down and waited for Camilla
Henderson.


Rhett Fennell's hands tightened on the arms of the
chair as he forced himself not to move. He'd come down
to the lobby at 6:30 p.m. to wait for a glimpse of the
woman with whom he'd waited six years to exact his
revenge. The deep-seated anger that had gnawed at him
day in and day out burned as hotly as it had the day
Denise Eaton walked out of his life and into the arms
of a man who'd gone from friend to enemy.

His mother had pleaded with him to let it go—forget about the two people he'd trusted—but he couldn't. It was the thirst for revenge that fueled the fire to propel him to get up every day to grow the business he would use to inflict Denise Eaton with the emotional pain he'd carried for longer than he wanted to remember, and bring Trey Chambers to his knees.

At exactly seven o'clock, he stood and counted the steps it would take to bring him face-to-face with her. A wry smile tilted the corners of his mouth. It was half a dozen—the same number of years since the fateful day that would forever be branded into his memory.

"Good evening, Ms. Eaton."

Denise froze, her breath catching in her throat and making it impossible for her to move. She heard the roaring in her head, fearful that she was going to faint when she registered the voice of the man she'd feared running into since moving to D.C. Rhett Fennell was the only man she knew who could shout without raising his voice.

Her lips parted and she expelled a lungful of air and the roaring stopped. Her head came up as if pulled by an invisible string. Standing less than a foot away was Rhett Fennell, the man with whom she'd fallen in love, given her heart, virginity and a promise to share her life and future with him.

He'd matured. His face was leaner, his black hair close-cropped and there was an intensity in the deep-set dark eyes that didn't look at her but through her. Rising on shaking knees, Denise extended her hand.

"It's good seeing you again, Rhett."

Rhett reached for the proffered hand, holding it firmly within his large grasp before releasing it. His impassive expression did not change as he stared at the heart-shaped face with the wide-set dark brown eyes, delicate nose and temptingly curved mouth that conjured up memories of what he'd been reduced to after they'd finished making love. It was her mouth and what came out of it that had enthralled him before he'd turned to see her face for the first time.

Denise had been blessed with the voice of a temptress. It was low, sultry and definitely had a triple-X rating. She was the only woman he'd known or met who'd been able to seduce him with *hello*. However, time had been more than kind to her. Although appearing slimmer than she had when they were in college together, nonetheless she was strikingly beautiful.

He forced a smile that stopped before it reached his eyes. "And, it's very nice seeing you again. How long has it been?"

Denise's eyes narrowed. She wanted to tell Garrett Fennell there was no reason to play mind games with her. He was brilliant. Everything he saw, heard or read he remembered, and it was his photographic memory that made him an outstanding student and astute businessman.

And he looked every inch the successful businessman in a tailored charcoal-gray suit, pale blue shirt, purple silk tie and black wingtips. Garrett Mason Fennell was the epitome of sartorial splendor.

She'd admitted to her cousin, Chandra Eaton-Tucker, that if she did run into Rhett again she would lose it. Well, she hadn't—even though she was becoming more uncomfortable with each passing second. She'd also confessed to Chandra that she hadn't gotten over her former lover and if she were completely honest with herself she would have to admit she would never get over him because she hadn't wanted to.

"Six years, Rhett."

Rhett angled his head. "Has it really been that long?"

"Yes, it has," Denise retorted sharply. Either he was feigning ignorance, or what they'd shared was just a blip in his memory. She glanced at her watch again. "I'd like to stay and reminisce with you, but I'm supposed to meet someone for dinner."

Rhett glanced around the lobby. "Is he here yet?"

"It's not a he, but a she."

"I hope you're not waiting for Camilla Henderson."

Denise stared at Rhett as if he'd suddenly grown a third eye. "You know Camilla Henderson?"

Rhett felt like a cat playing with a mouse he'd trapped and stunned, but was reluctant to kill. It was time he put an end to the charade and reveal his intent.

"She works for me. Unfortunately, she had an unforeseen situation where she couldn't be here, so you're going to have to deal with me tonight."

"You're involved with Capital Management Properties?"

"I've just taken over as CEO of CMP."

"You…you're responsible for the one hundred percent increase in rent on *my* child care center?"

Rhett's eyebrows lifted a fraction. "Aren't you being premature?"

"What the hell are you talking about?" Her voice had lowered as her temper escalated.

"Didn't you agree to meet with my chief financial officer to negotiate the terms of your center's lease renewal?"

"Yes, but—"

"Let's talk about it, Denise," Rhett said, interrupting

her. He cupped her elbow, steering her across the lobby. "I've reserved a table in The Lafayette."

Denise attempted to extricate her arm, but encountered resistance. She could not escape the fingers tightening like manacles. "You deceived me!"

Rhett stopped abruptly, as she plowed into his side. He turned toward her. "Spoken like someone who's quite familiar with the word."

"I didn't deceive you, Rhett."

"Save your breath, Denise. You're going to need it after you hear my business proposition."

"What kind of proposition?" Denise asked, unable to ignore the shudder swirling throughout her body. Rhett was making a business proposition when they had nothing in common other than he was now her landlord.

"We'll discuss it over dinner."

Denise went completely still, then managed to relax when Rhett rested his hand at the small of her back. It was as if nothing had changed, as if it'd been six hours instead of six years that had separated them.

# *Chapter 2*

However, if things between them *hadn't* changed she now would've been Denise Fennell and probably would've had at least one, if not, two children. Rhett, who was an only child, always talked about having a big family. When she'd asked him what he felt constituted a big family his reply had been a minimum of four children. They'd argued good-naturedly, she refusing to agree to push out four babies, while Rhett reminded her of how much fun it would be making babies.

Denise knew conjuring up images of the passionate encounters she'd had with Rhett would be detrimental to her emotional well-being. It had taken a long time to recover from his deceit and now that her life was on track she wanted nothing to derail it again.

"Your table is ready, Mr. Fennell."

Rhett's arm went around her waist, holding her close to his length. Denise was relieved she'd chosen to wear the stilettos. She was five-four in bare feet, and the additional four inches put her at eye level with Rhett's broad shoulder.

"How often do you eat here?" she asked him after he'd seated her.

"Enough," Rhett replied cryptically.

Denise stared across the small space of the table for two, her eyes taking in everything that made Rhett the confident man she'd loved selfishly. "How often is enough?" He'd greeted the maître d' and several of the waitstaff by name.

Rhett stared at Denise with lowered lids. He didn't want to believe she was more stunning than he'd remembered. The private investigator on his payroll had more than earned his salary. He made a mental note to give the man a generous year-end bonus. The former police officer had information on the teacher she probably hadn't remembered, or had chosen not to remember.

"I stay at the hotel whenever I have business in D.C."

A slight frown furrowed Denise's smooth forehead. Whenever she saw Garrett Fennell's name linked with a D.C.-based company in the business section of *The Washington Post,* she was under the impression that he still lived in his hometown.

"Where's home now?" she asked, staring at his firm mouth.

A hint of a smile found its way to Rhett's eyes. "I have a little place off the Chesapeake."

Resting her elbow on the table, Denise cupped her chin on the heel of her hand. "So you got your wish," she said in a quiet voice. "You always said you wanted to live on the water."

Rhett's expression changed, becoming somber. "Unfortunately, not all of my wishes were granted."

"What more could you have wanted, Rhett? You've become a successful entrepreneur, you have the home you wanted and—"

"You don't know what the hell you're talking about," he said, cutting her off.

Denise's arm came down and she sat back, her eyes never leaving the pair pinning her to the chair. He'd done it again. He had yelled at her without raising his voice. "If you talk to me like that again, I'm going to get up and walk out of here."

"You do that and you'll throw away everything you've worked so hard for. And knowing you like I believe I do, you won't do that just because someone said something you don't like."

"You're not someone, Rhett," she countered angrily. "Remember, we're not strangers."

"That's something I'll never forget, because you made certain of that."

Her eyes narrowed. "So, you're still blaming me for something you initiated and let get out of control." Rhett's reply was preempted when the waiter brought menus to the table.

"Would you like to order cocktails before I take your order, Mr. Fennell?"

"We'll have a bottle of champagne."

"Your usual, sir?"

"Yes, please."

Denise did not want to believe Rhett had ordered champagne without asking her beverage choice. "I don't want anything to drink because I'm driving," she said softly after the waiter had walked away.

Rhett smiled. "Don't worry. I'll make certain you get home safely."

"How are you going to do that?"

"I'll drive you home and then take a taxi back here."

"That's not necessary." It was enough that Rhett knew where she worked, and Denise didn't want him to know where she lived.

Picking up the menu, Rhett studied the entrées as Denise seethed inwardly. His success had made him not only arrogant but also rude. When they'd dated she rarely drank. Being underage was a factor and even when she'd reached the legal drinking age she'd discovered one drink usually left her feeling giddy.

"You've changed, Rhett."

"And you haven't?" he said, never taking his eyes off the menu.

"Yes, I have. I'm no longer the wide-eyed young girl who got to sleep with the smartest guy on campus."

Rhett's head came up as he slumped back in his chair. "You think what we'd had was all about sex, Denise?"

"What else was it, Rhett?" she asked, answering his question with her own. "Even you admitted you'd never connected with a woman the way you had with me."

Pressing his palms together, he brought his fingertips to his mouth. He'd fallen in love with Denise Eaton because of her outspokenness, passion *and* her ambition. Of all the women he'd met at Johns Hopkins, she'd been the most focused and driven. Even at eighteen she knew who she was and what she'd wanted for her future.

She was a Philadelphia Eaton, while he was the only child of a single mother who'd looked young enough to pass for his sister. Denise had grown up in a sprawling house on several acres with her attorney father and schoolteacher mother and an older brother. Her brother had attended the prestigious Citadel in Charleston, South Carolina, with the intention of becoming a professional soldier.

Meanwhile, he hadn't known his father, and whenever he'd asked Geraldine Fennell about him, she would say she didn't know. His mother didn't know the man who'd fathered him, and every time he walked the streets in his neighborhood he'd randomly searched the faces of men in an attempt to find one who he thought he looked like.

Gerri, as she was affectionately called by the few friends she'd held on to from her childhood, worked two jobs to send him to a boarding school twelve miles from their blighted neighborhood so he would get a quality education. Her sacrifice had paid off, because he'd been awarded full academic scholarships to Stanford, Howard University, Harvard and Johns Hopkins. Rhett had decided on the latter, because the scholarship included not only tuition but also books, room and board. The university was also close enough to D.C. so he could easily return home during school breaks.

The adage that there is a thin line between love and hate was evident after Denise dashed all of the plans they'd made for their future to crawl into bed with Trey Chambers. He'd wanted to hate her, but couldn't. He'd wanted to hurt her, but hadn't. Now the only thing he wanted was revenge—the sweetest revenge that he would exact in his own time, using his own methods.

"That was then."

"And this is now," she said softly.

"Yes, it is," Rhett said slowly as if measuring his words. "Speaking of now—how is your family?"

Denise, relieved to change the focus of the conversation from her and Rhett, smiled. "Thankfully, everyone's well."

"How's your brother?"

"Xavier has retired from active service. He went to Iraq a couple of years after 9/11 for two tours of duty. He was stateside for a while, and last year he was deployed again, this time to Afghanistan. A month before he was scheduled to return home he took a bullet to the leg that shattered his femur."

"What is he doing now?"

"He just got a teaching position at a military school in South Carolina, much to the relief of my mother, who went to church every day to light a candle that he wouldn't come back in a flag-draped casket."

Rhett had always liked Xavier. The career soldier had become the older brother he'd wished he had. "Are your parents well?"

"Very well," she said, smiling. "Daddy is now a state supreme court judge. Mom put in for early retirement, and now complains that she's bored out of her mind. All she does is cook and bake cakes."

"Your mother missed her calling."

"And that is?"

"She should've become a chef instead of a teacher." Whenever he'd gone to Philadelphia with Denise, her mother had prepared so much food that she'd invited every family member within a twenty-mile radius. Although he and Denise hadn't been engaged, the Eatons had unofficially adopted him into their family.

Denise's smile was dazzling. "I think you just gave me an idea, Rhett. When I speak to my mother I'm going to suggest she take some cooking classes."

Rhett's smile matched Denise's and for a brief moment he forgot why he was sitting across the table from her in a hotel restaurant. "Your mother is an incredible cook, unlike my mother, who still can't boil water."

A tender expression softened Denise's features when she remembered meeting Rhett's mother for the first time. Her greeting of "you're the daughter I always wanted" had resonated with her long after she and Rhett had driven back to Baltimore after a holiday weekend.

"How is your mother?"

"Believe it or not, she got married last year."

"I don't believe it. Your mother is so beautiful, and what I didn't understand was that men were practically genuflecting whenever they saw her, yet she wouldn't give any of them the time of day."

Rhett chuckled, the warm honeyed sound coming from deep within his chest. "She finally met someone who wasn't intimidated by her hostile glares and sharp tongue. Russ claims he chased her until she caught him. She used every excuse in the book as to why she wouldn't make a good wife, including her inability to cook, until he promised to hire a personal chef."

"Did he?" Denise asked.

"Yes. He made good on his promise and they have a cook who prepares their meals, so the only thing Mom has to do is heat them up in the oven or the microwave."

Denise wanted to tell Rhett his mother didn't have to learn to cook because she'd worked at a restaurant and brought food home. She also didn't tell him that six months ago she'd gone to see Geraldine Fennell, but neighbors told her Gerri had moved and hadn't left a forwarding address.

"I hope she's happy."

"She is," Rhett confirmed. "Once I convinced her to give up one of her jobs, she got her GED and eventually went online to get a liberal arts degree. She says she doesn't know what she's going to do with it, but earning a college degree is something she'd always wanted."

The sommelier approached the table with two flutes and a bottle of champagne in a crystal ice bucket. He poured a small amount into one flute, handed it to Rhett, and then filled both when he nodded his approval.

Rhett offered Denise the wineglass, their fingers touching. Holding his flute aloft, he gave her a long, penetrating look. "Here's to a successful business arrangement."

With wide eyes, Denise stared at him over the rim. "What business arrangement?" The query was barely a whisper.

He took a sip of the sparkling wine. "Drink up, Denise."

Her fingers tightened on the stem of the glass. "No. I'm not going to toast or drink to something I know nothing about."

Rhett set his glass down. He knew his dining partner well enough to know she wouldn't do anything she didn't want to do. "I want you to stand in as my hostess for the summer."

A soft gasp escaped Denise when she replayed Rhett's *business proposal* in her head. "You need a girlfriend?" There was a thread of incredulity in the question.

"No, Denise, I don't need a girlfriend. I broke up with my girlfriend a couple of months ago, and I'm not looking for another one. Unfortunately I've committed to quite a few social engagements this summer, and I need someone who will stand in as my date and hostess, providing your boyfriend doesn't object."

Clasping her hands together, she concealed their trembling under the table. "I don't have a boyfriend."

"That alleviates one obstacle."

She rolled her eyes at him. "Why don't you contact a dating service, Rhett? I'm certain they can find someone to your liking."

Leaning forward, Rhett's face suddenly went grim. "I don't do dating services."

Denise refused to relent. "Have you been in a monastery since we broke up?"

"Who I've slept with is none of your business," he retorted.

"I didn't ask who you were sleeping with, Garrett Mason Fennell. I said—"

"I know what you said. You have a choice, Miss Eaton. Either it's yes or no." He knew she was upset because she'd called him by his full name.

"What are my options?"

"If you say no, then you'll receive a lease renewal agreement doubling your current monthly rent."

Denise blinked, unable to believe what she'd heard. "That's blackmail!"

"I call it negotiating, Denise. You want something from me, and I'm offering you a way out of your dilemma. I could've said I wanted you to sleep with me."

"That's sexual harassment."

"Call it whatever you want," Rhett said quietly. "You have exactly one minute to give me an answer, or the deal is off the table."

"And if I say yes?" Denise felt as if someone had put their fingers around her throat, slowly squeezing the life out of her.

Rhett knew he had Denise on the ropes when he saw her shoulders slump. And, like a shark drawn to the smell of blood, he went in for the kill.

"You give me the next three and a half months of your life and I'll offer you a two-year lease with a ten percent increase."

"Make it three years and six percent," she countered.

"Three years, eight percent, and that's my final offer."

Denise felt as if she'd won a small victory. Picking up her flute, she extended it. "Deal," she crooned, touching glasses. She took a sip of champagne. "Why me, and not some other woman?" she asked, seeing his smug expression.

Rhett lowered his gaze, staring at the back of his left hand. "I don't have time to tutor someone about social etiquette and protocol."

"How often will I have to stand in as your hostess?"

"Every weekend."

"Every weekend?" she repeated. "You're kidding me, aren't you?"

"No, I'm not kidding you, Denise. We'll either entertain here in D.C., or on Cape St. Claire."

The waiter's sudden appearance to take their order was the only thing that stopped Denise from spewing the acid-laced response poised on the tip of her tongue. She narrowed her eyes, glaring at Rhett when she wanted to wipe the smirk off his face. Crossing her arms over her chest, she counted slowly in an attempt to control her temper.

"It can't be every weekend," she said when they were alone again.

Rhett angled his head. "Is your business open on the weekend?"

She rolled her eyes at him. "No."

"It can't be because of a man, because you said you didn't have a boyfriend."

"Boyfriend or not, I still have other obligations."

Rhett glanced up, annoyance and frustration welling up within him. If he wasn't careful, his plan would backfire and that was something he wanted to avoid, given the risks he'd taken to exact revenge from Denise Eaton for turning his world upside down. His most ruthless business foes hadn't been able to affect him the way she had.

He'd designed his retribution as carefully as he studied a company on the brink of bankruptcy before he stepped in to take it over. Rhett had been hard-pressed not to shout at the top of his lungs when his investigator uncovered that Denise had opened a child care center in D.C., and on property his company had recently purchased from a developer who'd been forced to abandon his plan to revitalize four square blocks of commercial real estate after the housing market bottomed out. He'd paid the developer a little more than half the fair market value for the property, and the developer took the check and thanked him profusely.

His game plan included seducing Denise back into his bed, then walking out on her as she had walked out on him. The only difference was there wouldn't be a woman waiting for him as there had been for her years ago.

"What type of other social obligations?"

"I have two fundraisers—one in June and the other in August. I'm also involved in planning my cousin Belinda's baby shower."

Belinda Eaton-Rice was due at the end of the month and the family had decided that a get-together over the three-day weekend would provide an opportune setting for a baby shower.

"Does she know about the shower?"

Denise smiled for the first time since she'd agreed to go along with Rhett's unorthodox proposal. "No. My parents are supposedly hosting the get-together, and that will give Griffin time to drive Belinda to Philly while the rest of us decorate their house in Paoli. Once they arrive, Griffin will have to come up with an excuse why they have to return to Paoli."

Rhett lifted his eyebrows a fraction. "I must say I was quite surprised when I'd heard that Griffin Rice had married Belinda Eaton."

It was Denise's turn to raise her eyebrows. "How did you hear about it?"

"Keith Ennis."

"You know Keith?" Denise asked. The Philadelphia Phillies ballplayer was a sports superstar. As Keith's agent, Griffin had helped the naturally gifted athlete from a poor Baltimore neighborhood to superstar status with a five-year multimillion-dollar contract, along with high-profile endorsement deals.

"We'd shared a table at a Baltimore fundraiser, and I overheard him tell someone he was going to be a groomsman in his agent's wedding. When I heard him mention Belinda Eaton I knew then it was your cousin."

"Griffin and Belinda shocked everyone when they announced they were getting married," Denise said, smiling. "I'd always thought they couldn't stand each other." She sobered. "Griffin losing his brother and Belinda her sister brought them closer together after they became guardians for Donna and Grant's twin daughters."

"I've always liked your family, Denise."

She nodded, scrunching up her nose. "I kind of like them, too. In fact, Chandra asked me about you."

"And what did you tell her?"

"She'd asked if I'd run into you now that I'm living in D.C. and I told her I hadn't."

Rhett leaned closer. "That is, until now," he said softly.

Denise stared at Rhett. There was something in his eyes that communicated he was mocking her. A sixth sense wouldn't let her feel comfortable about their reunion. It wasn't coincidental that he'd happened to purchase the building where she'd set up New Visions Childcare. His reputation as a ruthless corporate raider had earned him the reputation as one of thirty under thirty rising stars in *Beltway Business Review.* At twenty-eight, Garrett Fennell was touted as the Warren Buffett of his generation. She knew there was only one way to find out what he was up to, and that was for her to play the same game.

"Do you have anything planned for the Memorial Day weekend?"

Rhett drained the flute. "I have an invitation to a neighbor's cookout on Sunday. Why?"

"Belinda's shower is scheduled for Saturday afternoon, and I'd like you to come with me. After that, I'm all yours for the rest of the weekend." Denise knew she'd shocked Rhett with her suggestion when he stared at her as if he'd never seen her before.

"You want *me* to hang out with your family?"

"Of course," she said flippantly. "I'm certain they'll welcome you back with open arms."

A beat passed before Rhett spoke again. "What did you tell your parents about our breakup?"

Denise closed her eyes, recalling the meeting with her parents. She'd managed not to break down when they'd asked when she and Rhett were getting married.

She opened her eyes, her gaze fusing with the man. Despite her silent protest, she still loved and would always love him. He'd deceived her with another woman and she still couldn't hate him.

"I told them the truth." Her voice was barely a whisper. "I said I'd fallen out of love with you."

Reaching across the table, Rhett took her hand, increasing the pressure when she tried to escape him. "Do you hate me, Denise?" The second hand dial on his timepiece made a full revolution as they stared at each other.

"No, Rhett, I don't hate you."

Exhaling a breath at the same time he let go of Denise's hand, Rhett stared at a spot over her shoulder. "If that's the case, then I'll go with you to Belinda's baby shower."

# Chapter 3

Denise unlocked the door to her apartment, tossed her keys and handbag on the side table in the entryway and kicked off her shoes. In her stocking-covered feet, she headed for the bedroom.

Rhett hadn't driven her home, because she'd only drunk half a glass of champagne. However, he'd walked her to her car, waited until she'd maneuvered away from the curb and turned the corner.

She was angry and annoyed. Her anger was directed at Rhett for using what amounted to blackmail to get her to do his bidding. His excuse that he needed her to double as his date and hostess was so transparent she had almost laughed in his face.

She was annoyed at herself for inviting him to her cousin's baby shower. His presence would literally open a Pandora's box of questions to which she had few or no answers.

The blinking red light on the telephone console on the bedside table indicated she had a message. Reaching for the cordless receiver, she punched in the numbers to retrieve her voice mail. The voice of Chandra Eaton-Tucker came through the earpiece:

*"Denise, this is Chandra. Please call me when you get this message. I don't care how late it is when you get in. Call me."*

Denise dialed the Philadelphia area code, then Chandra's number. The phone rang twice before there was a break in the connection. "This is Chandra."

"Hey. I hope I'm not calling too late."

Denise walked over to the window and drew the drapes. She sat on an off-white upholstered chair, and propped her feet on a matching footstool. She'd decorated the bedroom as a calming retreat. A bay window had become a seating area with the chair, footstool and off-white silk drapery and sheers.

A queen-size bed with white and beige bed linens, a padded bench covered with silk throw pillows in shades ranging from chocolate to cream was set up for an alcove that had become a second seating area. The stenciled floral design on the double dresser and lingerie chest matched the area rug.

"Preston has been locked in his office for the past two days revising his latest play."

"Does he come out to eat?"

"Rarely," Chandra said. "I usually don't intrude when he gets into what he calls the 'zone.' Now, back to why I called you. I got a set of keys from Griffin today, so we'll be able to let ourselves in."

"What time do you want me to meet you?" Denise asked her cousin.

"Meet me in Paoli any time before ten. I know

that means your leaving D.C. early, but I want to get everything decorated before one o'clock."

"There's something you should know," Denise said after a pause.

"What, Denise?"

"I'm bringing someone with me."

"Good! The more the merrier."

"You don't understand, Chandra."

"What's not to understand, Denise? You have a date."

An audible sigh filled the room as she stared at the lighted wall sconce in the sitting alcove. "What if my date is Rhett Fennell? Are you still there, Chandra?" she asked when silence came through the earpiece.

"I'm here. When did you start seeing him again?"

"Tonight we had dinner together."

Denise knew she had to alert Chandra that she was coming with Rhett, because not to would prove embarrassing to all involved and knowing Chandra she knew she would tell the other family members that Rhett was back in her life. Although it was just for the summer, he would still be a part of her life until she fulfilled the terms of their business arrangement.

"Do you want me to tell the others that he's coming?"

"There's no need to send out an APB."

Chandra laughed. "I'll try to be subtle."

It was Denise's turn to laugh. "You wouldn't know subtle if it stood on your chest, Mrs. Tucker."

"You know you're wrong, Denise Eaton."

"Hang up, Chandra."

"Good night."

Denise ended the call, pressed her head to the back of the chair and closed her eyes. She couldn't believe she'd allowed herself to be victimized by a man who held the future of her business venture in his grasp. Rhett knew the importance of reliable and quality day care. He'd grown up with latchkey kids who were left home alone because their parents had to work and couldn't afford to pay someone to look after their children. Social workers from children's services made regular visits to his neighborhood to follow up on complaints stemming from abuse and neglect of children who were unsupervised at night and into the early morning hours. Rhett had been one of the luckier children because his aunt babysat him until he was school-age.

She opened her eyes, struggling not to let the tears filling her eyes spill over. She'd accused Rhett of blackmail and sexual harassment, while he'd called it negotiating. The only saving grace was they wouldn't sleep together. Making love to Rhett Fennell was akin to smoking crack. The addiction was instantaneous.

Forcing herself to rise from the comfy chair, Denise went through the motions of undressing. Then she walked into the en suite bathroom to remove her makeup. Twenty minutes later she touched the switch, turning off the wall sconce and floor lamp. Her eyelids were drooping slightly when she pulled back the comforter and slipped between cool, crisp sheets. Reaching over, she turned off the lamp on the bedside table, and this time when she closed her eyes she didn't open them again until a sliver of light poured in through the octagonal window over the sitting area.

Rhett massaged his forehead with his fingertips as he compared the bottom line for three years of profit and loss statements for Chambers Properties, Ltd. A steady decline in profits was an obvious indicator that the company was ripe for the picking.

After reuniting with Denise Eaton, he'd thrown himself into his work with the voracity of a starving man at a banquet. Work and more work had not diminished his anxiety at being unable to get her out of his head.

During the walk back to the hotel, after having made certain she was safely in her car, Rhett had replayed the two hours they'd spent together. Even when he'd executed what some had called his "sucker punch" takeover, he hadn't felt as ashamed as he had now. His quest for revenge had gone beyond what he deemed ethical. He'd used his money and the power that went along with it to intimidate and bully a woman who'd sacrificed her time and money to provide essential services to a low-income and working-class community.

Although he'd threatened to double the rent for the child care facility, Rhett knew he never would've gone through with it. After all, he wasn't that far removed from his humble roots to ignore the importance of adequate child care. He was luckier than most of the children from his neighborhood because his maternal aunt had looked after him while his mother worked long hours waiting tables.

When he was six years old, Geraldine Fennell had enrolled him in Marshall Foote Academy, a prestigious boarding school in northern Virginia, where he'd returned home during the summer months and holidays. He'd studied harder than any other boy at the prep school, and after a year his mother had been able to qualify for financial aid. For every grade of ninety and above, the tuition for that term had been waived.

Rhett had learned early in life that he was smart. But he hadn't realized how smart he actually was until it had come time for exams. One of his instructors had accused him of cheating because he'd written verbatim the answer he'd read in his textbook. It was only after Geraldine had been summoned to the school for a conference with the teacher and headmaster that they had become aware of his photographic memory. He was able to recall whole paragraphs from textbooks without thinking about it.

It had been the first and only time he'd seen his mother lose her temper. And it had been the only time he'd forgotten some of the words she'd flung at the red-faced men. Once they'd apologized profusely, Geraldine had returned to D.C., Rhett had been escorted back to his dormitory and the headmaster had chastised the instructor for embarrassing him and jeopardizing the academy's reputation with unsubstantiated allegations when he'd accused their best student of cheating.

Attending the academy had afforded him the opportunity for a quality education. He'd also managed to escape the social problems that plagued his poor urban neighborhood.

Yes, he'd made it out *and* he'd made a difference. But the differences were quiet, subtle. And with every company he took over, Rhett always looked after the employees. Those who wanted out he offered a generous severance package. Those who didn't, he created positions for them—even if he had to reduce their salaries. The rationale was at least they had a paycheck.

The buzz of the intercom interrupted his reverie. "Yes, Tracy."

"Your uncle is here."

Rhett smiled. "Tell him I'll be right out." He took a quick glance at the clock on his desk. "I'll probably be gone for the rest of the day. Take messages and if there's anything you can't handle, then call me on my cell."

"No problem, Rhett," said his executive assistant.

He'd hired Tracy Powell when his office had been nothing more than a twelve-by-twelve second bedroom in his apartment after he'd earned an MBA from Wharton business school. He'd purchased two used desks, installed a telephone line separate from his personal one and he and the part-time bookkeeper/ secretary/receptionist grew a company from two to fourteen employees.

After two years, Rhett rented space in an office building in downtown D.C., and now he owned a four-story town house blocks from Dupont Circle. The first three floors were occupied by his various holding companies. And when renovations on the fourth floor were completed Rhett would move into what would become his private apartment. His decision to live in the same building where he worked was because he'd found himself spending more time there than he had at his condominium. He'd sold the condo and had temporarily moved into the hotel while the contractor renovated the space.

What he constantly reminded himself was that other than his mother, he had no family. His grandparents were dead and so was the aunt who'd looked after him. There was only he and his mother, who'd found happiness with a sixty-year-old widower who adored her.

Rhett knew his reluctance to settle down with a woman stemmed from his relationship with Denise Eaton. The first time he'd slept with her he knew he wanted her to be the only woman in his life. What he hadn't known at the time was that she wouldn't be. There had been women after Denise—more than he'd willingly admit—to fill up the empty hours or to slake his sexual frustration.

Then everything had changed when a woman had accused him of leading her on, that she'd expected a commitment that would eventually lead to marriage. He'd made a decision not to date or sleep with women. It was during this time that he'd been forced to reexamine his wanton behavior and acknowledge his selfishness.

Women were not his playthings. They were not receptacles for his lust or frustration. They wanted more than a *slam bam thank you ma'am*. When he'd finally told his mother about the revolving door of women in and out of his life, her comeback had been he should think of them as his sister—did he want a man to treat her with a total disregard for her feelings? The analogy had been enough for him to stop his self-destructive behavior.

Rolling down and buttoning the cuffs of his shirt, Rhett reached for the jacket to his suit and walked out of his office. He nodded in the direction of the man lounging on a leather chair in the waiting alcove outside his office.

Tracy Powell peered over her half-glasses, a profusion of salt-and-pepper braids framing her smooth gold-brown face. She couldn't understand why the rumpled-looking older man hadn't taken a hint from his young nephew and put on something that didn't look as if it had just come out of the washing machine.

"Enjoy your lunch," she called out to the two men.

Rhett gave her a wink. "Thank you."

He walked with Eli Oakes to the elevator, taking it to the street level. Moments after stepping out into the bright sunlight, they exchanged a handshake. Eli wasn't his uncle, but a private investigator. When he'd met Eli for the first time, Rhett thought of him as kind of a black Columbo. Eli even wore a wrinkled trench coat during cooler, rainy weather. The former police officer admitted to being forty-seven, a confirmed bachelor and a recovering alcoholic. Tall and gangly with smooth sable-brown skin, the man's innocuous appearance was a foil for a sharp mind that noted details most people were likely to overlook.

"Where do you want to eat?"

Eli put on a pair of sunglasses, then ran a hand over his stubbly pate. "I had a big breakfast, so I don't need anything too heavy."

Rhett rested a hand on the older man's shoulder. "There's a new restaurant on Massachusetts that features salads and wraps and vegetarian dishes. We can try it if you want."

Eli smiled. "Let's try it."

"What do you have for me?" Rhett asked after he and Eli gave the waitress their orders.

Reaching into the pocket of his jacket, Eli pulled out a folded sheet of paper. "See for yourself." He pushed it across the table.

Rhett unfolded the page of type. His expression didn't change as he read the information the investigator had come up with on Trey Chambers. "He's a busy boy," he murmured. "No wonder his business is in the toilet."

Eli picked up a glass of sweet tea, taking a long swallow. "What I didn't include in that report is that Chambers spends a lot of time at the track."

Rhett digested this information as he counted the number of boards on which Trey Chambers either chaired or was a member. What surprised him was Eli's claim that Trey had a gambling problem. When they were in college together he hadn't remembered the business major gambling. Even when coeds were placing bets during March Madness, Trey hadn't participated.

"Is he winning or losing?"

Eli shrugged his shoulders under his jacket. "Both. He made a bundle betting on the Derby and Preakness, but we'll have to see what he does with the Belmont Stakes."

"Trey was never much of a gambler."

A sly smile parted the lips of the man whose decorated law enforcement career had ended after he'd been injured in a hit-and-run when he'd gone out early one morning to buy the newspaper. He'd lain in a coma for several months; when he'd emerged he submitted his retirement papers and went into private investigation. "Trey's daddy is no longer collecting wives, but horses. That could explain Junior's sudden interest in the ponies."

Rhett wanted to tell Eli that if the Chambers were winning at the track, they weren't putting it back into their real estate business. Chambers Properties owned large parcels of land in Baltimore and D.C., and there was one tract not far from Baltimore Harbor that Chambers wanted. Rhett, also interested in the property, had submitted a bid.

The waitress approached the table, setting down a plate with a tuna salad with sprouts on a bed of lettuce for Eli and a bowl of Caesar salad for Rhett.

Over lunch, the topic of conversation changed to sports—baseball and the upcoming football season. The two men talked about trades and drafts, becoming more animated when they argued good-naturedly about teams they predicted would win the World Series and Super Bowl. Most of the lunch crowd had thinned out when Rhett paid the check and slid an envelope across the table.

Eli picked up the envelope, peering into its contents. "What's up with the cash?" Rhett usually gave him a check as payment for his services.

"Think of it as a mid-year bonus."

Lines of consternation were etched into Eli's forehead. "A bonus for what?"

Rhett wanted to tell the man to take the money and stop asking so many questions, but he knew once a cop always a cop. He didn't want Eli to think he was trying to set him up, which was why he always paid him with a check and at the end of the year issued a 1099 for his personal services.

"It's a little extra for reuniting me with my old girlfriend."

Eli's expression brightened. "If that's the case, then I'll humbly accept your mid-year bonus."

Backing away from the table, the men walked out of the restaurant, going in opposite directions. Rhett walked back to where he'd parked his car. Instead of driving to the hotel, he headed in the opposite direction. A quarter of an hour later, he maneuvered into the parking lot across the street from New Visions Childcare.

"How long will you be gone?" the attendant asked.

"Less than half an hour," Rhett said, handing the man the keys to his late-model Mercedes Benz sedan.

Crossing the street, he opened the door to the one-story brick building and walked into a reception area. Recessed lighting illuminated the space with a warm glow while the calming green paint with an alphabet border added a festive touch. Rhett had also noticed several security cameras were positioned inside and outside the facility.

A young woman sitting behind a glassed partition was on the phone arguing with someone who wanted to pick up a child, but didn't have authorization. "I'm sorry, Mr. Hawkins, but rules are rules. If you submit official documentation from the court, then we'll be able to release your son to you. You have a good day, too." She stuck out her tongue at the telephone console before realizing someone was watching her.

Rhett smiled as she slid back the glass. "I'm here to see Ms. Denise Eaton."

The receptionist, who had long airbrushed nails, gave him a bored look. "Is she expecting you?"

"No, she isn't. Can you please let her know Garrett Fennell would like to see her?"

"Ms. Eaton usually won't see anyone without an appointment."

"I'm certain she'll see me." There was a ring of confidence in the statement.

"What's your name again?"

"Garrett Fennell."

He stared at the woman's long nails, which reminded him of talons, as she tapped the buttons of the telephone console, and spoke quietly into her headset. She pushed another button. "Please have a seat, Mr. Fennell. Ms. Eaton will be with you shortly."

Rhett sat on a decorative wrought-iron back bench and thumbed through a magazine from a stack on a low side table. He smiled at the picture of an infant staring back at him on the glossy cover. Flipping through the magazine, he found an article about coping with temper tantrums. Halfway through the article, the receptionist told him Ms. Eaton was now available to see him.

He walked toward the door with a sign that said you

had to see the receptionist before being buzzed in. He pushed open the door when the buzzer sounded, coming face-to-face with a very different Denise Eaton.

## Chapter 4

When Denise left Rhett standing on the curb, she hadn't expected to see him again until Saturday. Less than twenty-four hours later he had surprised her again.

"Have you come to renege on our deal?"

Denise had spoken so softly Rhett had to strain to hear what she was saying. "Is that what you want?" he asked. "You want out?"

"Did I say I wanted out?" Denise found it hard to breathe. She was standing in a hallway, less than two feet from Rhett Fennell, whose presence seemed to suck the air from her lungs. She lowered her gaze rather than let him see her lusting after him. And that was exactly what she'd fantasized about the night before. She'd gone to bed thinking of Rhett, which was enough to trigger an erotic dream. When she awoke, it was to a pounding heartbeat and a pulsing between her legs that left her wet and moaning in frustration.

"Come to my office, and we'll talk."

Denise had invited Rhett to her office when what she'd wanted was to show him the door. They had struck a deal to see each other on weekends only.

Rhett noticed the gentle sway of Denise's hips in a pair of black cropped stretch pants. He knew she was tense because her back was ramrod straight and both hands at her side were balled into fists. The casual slacks, sleeveless white blouse and black sandals with a wedge heel made her look more approachable than she had the night before. The blue dress reminded him of an ice queen—look but don't touch. And he hadn't touched her except to cradle her elbow.

Even her hairstyle was different. Instead of the bun, which he'd found much too severe for her age and delicate features, a narrow headband pulled her glossy curls off her face. When they were in school together she'd always worn a short hairstyle.

Rhett felt the flesh between his thighs come to life when the image of her hair spread across his pillow popped into his head. Just as quickly, it went away, leaving him breathing heavier and with an ache in his groin. A muscle twitched in his jaw as he clenched his teeth. Fortunately for him, Denise was in front of him or she wouldn't have been able to miss his hard-on straining against his fly. As surreptitiously as he could, he buttoned his jacket, concealing the bulge.

"How much work did you have to do to this place before you were able to open?" He had to talk. Say anything to keep his mind off Denise's slim, yet curvy body. They walked past closed doors to offices for the center's social worker, dietician and business manager. Nameplates identified each person and their position.

Denise slowed when she came to an open area with

eight round tables, each with seating for six. As in the reception area, she'd decided against chairs, opting instead for benches. Several skylights, potted plants, ferns and ficus trees provided a parklike atmosphere.

"Not too much," she threw over her shoulder as she opened the door to her office. Her name and position were etched on the nameplate affixed to the door. "The contractor had to patch up a few holes before he could paint. The previous owner had replaced the roof three years ago, so that saved me at least thirty grand."

Stepping aside, Denise let Rhett precede her into the room that at one time had been her second home. She'd come in at dawn to let the workmen in and occasionally slept on an inflatable bed she'd put away in a closet. The center was equipped with three full bathrooms, each with a shower and two half-baths in the nursery and classrooms for children, ranging in age from two to five.

"Please sit down, Rhett." Denise gestured toward a love seat in a soft neutral shade. She sat in a matching one facing him. She crossed one leg over the other, bringing his gaze to linger on the rose-pink polish on her toes. "Would you like something to eat or drink? We've just finished giving the children their lunch, so the kitchen is still open."

"No, thank you. I just ate."

He glanced around Denise's office. It reflected her personality with plants lining a window ledge. Her desk was an old oak top from another generation, a Tiffany-style desk lamp, a fireplace mantel filled with different size candles. Three of the four walls in her office were brick, the remaining one covered with framed prints of children from around the world.

Denise stared at Rhett through lowered lashes. To say

he looked delicious was an understatement. Today he wore a dark blue suit with a maroon-colored silk tie and white shirt. He looked nothing like the college student who'd favored jeans, pullover sweaters or sweatshirts. At that time, Rhett owned just one suit, which he only wore on special occasions.

"How old is that desk?"

Rhett's question caught Denise off guard. She didn't know why he'd come to the center, but she was willing to bet it had nothing to do with the furnishings. "It's quite old."

He smiled. "How old is quite old?"

"I'm not selling it, Rhett."

His eyebrows lifted. "Why don't you wait for me to make an offer."

"Offer all you want, I'm not selling."

Rhett angled his head, staring at the antique desk. "Have you had it appraised?"

She nodded. "Appraised and insured. It belonged to my grandfather who got it from a client who'd lost all of his assets in the crash of '29. The desk and several other pieces of furniture were payment for a criminal case my grandfather had taken on and won for him. My father inherited it from his father. He gave up his practice once he was appointed to the bench, and I quickly put in my bid for the desk."

"Who else wanted it?" Rhett asked.

"Every lawyer in the family pulled out their check-books, claiming it should go to someone practicing law, not a schoolteacher."

"Ouch," Rhett drawled, smiling. "That's definitely a shot across the bow."

Denise sucked her teeth. "Yeah, right. I was quick

to tell them the desk belonged to *my* father, and as his baby girl I was entitled to it."

"No, you didn't pull the baby-girl card."

"Whatever works, Rhett."

He sobered. "Speaking of whatever works, I'd like you to give me a tour of the facility."

"Why?" she countered. "Are you thinking of becoming an investor?"

Denise regretted the question as soon as it rolled off her tongue. It was enough that Rhett owned the building and the land on which New Visions Childcare sat, but she didn't need him to own a percentage of her business.

"Do you need an investor, Denise?"

"No," she said much too quickly. "My revenues are enough to support the day care operation."

"Do you have money put aside?"

"Yes." And she did. The monies she would get from the sale of her co-op would become her emergency fund. Denise had promised herself that she wouldn't use her personal funds unless it was a dire emergency. So far, she'd been able to keep that promise.

"Good for you." Rhett stood up, extended his hand and pulled Denise gently to her feet. "My initial reason for coming was to talk to you about this weekend."

"You could've called me, Rhett. After all, I did give you my number."

"I was in the neighborhood, so I decided to drop by."

He hadn't lied to Denise. He'd come to this section of D.C. to tour the neighborhood and see what was needed to upgrade the quality of life for the people who lived there. His company owned four square blocks designated for commercial use; the urban planner on his staff had suggested he drive around the neighborhood to survey the area before he made his decision about redevelopment.

"What are you doing, Rhett? Taking stock of your assets?"

Rhett knew Denise was spoiling for a confrontation because he'd coerced her into being his escort for the summer. She could've called his bluff and said no, but she hadn't. Despite their very intimate past, she still hadn't known him that well. If she had, then she would've believed him rather than Trey when he'd told her that he hadn't been sleeping with other women. And if she had truly believed him when he confessed to loving her, she wouldn't have ended up in bed with Trey.

He hadn't purchased the real estate to jack up the rents, as he'd threatened to do with New Visions, but to improve the property and the quality of life for the residents.

Rhett wasn't *that* far removed from the neighborhood in which he'd grown up not to recognize the importance of adequate child care. It provided a safe haven for the children of working parents and those who were trying to pursue their education and thereby better themselves and their families. However, Denise had fallen into a carefully planned trap.

He took a step, bringing him close enough for her chest to touch his. "Which assets do you speak of?"

Denise hadn't realized the double entendre until it was too late. Her lips parted at the same time Rhett angled his head, brushing his mouth over hers. His hands came up and he took her face, holding it gently as if he feared she would shatter if he let her go.

Slowly, deliberately, he caressed instead of kissing

her mouth, seeking to allay her fears that he wanted to dismantle what she'd worked so hard to establish. He kissed her because it was something he'd wanted to do the moment he saw her walk across the lobby of the Hay-Adams hotel.

Tiptoeing, Denise pressed her lips closer. Rhett's mouth brushed hers like a butterfly fluttering over her lips. She wanted more, much more, but she knew they couldn't and wouldn't go back in time.

She and Rhett had been caught up in a magical world where love and passion were indistinguishable. They'd eaten together, studied together, made love to each other and spent countless hours planning a future that included marriage and children.

However, four years of togetherness ended abruptly when the rumor floating around the university that Garrett Fennell was sleeping with her and another student was no longer a rumor but real when Denise opened the door to her boyfriend's dorm room to find a naked woman asleep in his bed. In that instant, the love she'd known and felt for Rhett disappeared. She'd left as quietly as she'd come, walking out of the building and out of Rhett's life.

"Don't! Please, Rhett."

Rhett froze, his gaze meeting and fusing with Denise's. There was something in her eyes he recognized as fear and he wondered whether he'd put it there. He dipped his head to kiss her again, but her hands pressed against his chest stopped him.

"What's wrong, Denise?"

A rush of heat singed Denise's face *and* body when she realized the enormity of what had just taken place. "You coming here unannounced and then kissing me when someone could've walked in on us. That's what's wrong," she spat out.

Smiling, Rhett pushed his hands into the pockets of his suit trousers to keep from reaching for her again. Anger had replaced the fear, and he remembered Denise being most passionate whenever she was angry. Memories of their makeup sex were permanently branded into his head.

"The next time I come I'll make certain to make an appointment beforehand. And I promise never to kiss you again in your office."

Denise saw the beginnings of a smirk. If she was going to be angry at anyone, then it had to be at herself. She'd learned never to challenge Rhett Fennell because he would accept the challenge and win.

He'd waged a silent and bloodless battle when he'd outlined the conditions for renewing her lease—leaving her with little or no recourse, and she was forced to accept his terms. Rhett had called it negotiating, while to her it was still a subtle form of blackmail.

The residents in the neighborhood needed the child care center, she wanted to make certain it remained open, and it wasn't as if she had a horde of men lining up outside her door to take her out.

What Denise hadn't wanted to think about was *if* she had had a boyfriend would Rhett have proposed the same game plan. Then she'd recalled him saying, "I need someone who will stand in as my date and hostess, provided your boyfriend doesn't object," and she'd answered her own question. It would not have made a difference.

"Please give me a few minutes, and I'll take you around to see the facility."

Walking on stiff legs, Denise went into the private

bathroom and shut the door. The image staring back at her in the mirror over the sink was one she didn't recognize.

"I don't know if I can do this," she whispered. If Rhett hadn't ended the kiss when he did, she probably would've asked for more—and more translated into her begging him to make love to her.

When she and Rhett shared a bed for the first time it had been *her* first time. Denise knew she'd shocked him, because she hadn't told him she was a virgin. What she hadn't wanted was for him to feel guilty and continue to see her out of a perverse sense of obligation.

However, he did continue to date her. It was another month before they made love again, and she'd experienced her first orgasm. Making love with Rhett was always good. Makeup sex was even better. It was the memories of their lovemaking, the plans they'd made for a life beyond college, that had lingered with her after she'd graduated and returned to Philadelphia.

It had taken more than a year for her to acknowledge what she'd had with Rhett was over and she had to move on with her life. She'd gotten back into the dating scene when she and several teachers at the school where she'd taught met regularly at a downtown Philly club on Friday nights. Denise had refused to date any of the male teachers with whom she worked, but she had met a software analyst at one of the weekly social mixers. They'd played telephone tag for several weeks before connecting.

Denise had liked Kevin enough to go out with him for three months. They'd slept together once. Days later she had been filled with guilt because she'd compared Kevin to Rhett, and the former fell far short of satisfying her. Kevin had seemed to get the picture without her having to connect the dots, and they had mutually agreed to stop seeing each other.

"Denise, are you all right in there?" asked Rhett outside the closed door.

"I'm good. Just give me a few more minutes."

*When did you become such an astute liar?* Denise mused, as she splashed cold water on her face. She patted her face with a soft towel, then opened the chest over the sink and took out a small jar with powder that matched her skin tone. She shook out a minute amount on a brush and applied the powder to her face. Within seconds her face had a rich, healthy glow. A coat of mascara to her lashes and lip gloss rounded out her mini-makeover. Denise ran her fingers through her hair, fluffing up the curls before she washed her hands.

*It's amazing what a new do, a new outfit and a little makeup can do to lift a woman's spirit.* Denise smiled in spite of the situation in which she'd found herself. "Thank you, Mom," she whispered.

Paulette Eaton's manifesto had served her well on many occasions. She didn't have a new do or outfit, but a little color on her face had done the trick. When she emerged from the bathroom she was emotionally ready to deal with the likes of Rhett Fennell.

Her eyes were smiling and her step light as she reached for a lanyard with her picture ID, then led him out of her office. "This area of the center is called the administrative section. Whenever we have staff meetings, or something when we invite the parents and siblings of the children enrolled here, we hold them out here."

"It looks like a park," Rhett said.

"We wanted it to look like a park with the trees and benches," Denise explained. "I've ordered an indoor waterfall and one of our board members gave the center a gift of a flat-screen television he'd won in a raffle. A technician is expected in before the end of the week to mount it on that wall." She pointed to a wall where anyone sitting at the tables would be able to view it.

"This place is so quiet. Where are the children?"

"It's nap time, so most of them are probably asleep."

"How long do they nap?"

"From twelve thirty to two. At two we get them up and give them a little snack. From three o'clock on, they're picked up by family members." She swiped her ID along a device on the door leading to the area where the children were sleeping. "Even though we have state-of-the-art security with cameras and an alarm that is connected directly to the local police station, we do everything possible to ensure the safety of our children."

"I have to assume everyone is buzzed in."

Denise nodded. "Employees must swipe in and out, and parents and those designated to pick up their children are buzzed in and out. We tell our parents over and over that if custodial arrangements change, then we must know about it immediately. If a woman breaks up with her boyfriend or husband and she doesn't want them to pick up her child or children, or if there is an order of protection or change in custody, then we must be notified like yesterday."

She stopped at a set of double doors, pushing one open. "This is our kitchen and Miss Jessie is our cook and dietician. Ms. Cox, this is Mr. Fennell."

Rhett nodded to the petite woman wearing a pale green uniform, hairnet and garish orange clogs. "Ms. Cox."

Jessie Cox smiled, then went back to slicing fruit for the afternoon snack. The industrial kitchen was outfitted with stainless-steel sinks and appliances. The refrigerators and walk-in freezers were also equipped with security devices.

Reaching for his hand, Denise led Rhett out of the kitchen. "Ms. Cox has started a dialogue with the parents about proper nutrition for their children. A few of our children are overweight, but after a few months they begin dropping the pounds."

Rhett noticed Denise always referred to the children as *our children,* and he wondered if she'd substituted the children at the facility for the ones they may have had if they'd stayed together.

"How many meals do you serve here?" he asked.

"Breakfast, lunch and an afternoon snack."

"What time do you open?"

"The facility opens at six, but parents can't drop off their children until seven. We close at six, but will stay open as late as seven. After seven, the parents will have to pick up their children at the police station."

"What if they're delayed?"

"If they call us, then usually someone will stay later than seven. It's something I don't advertise or encourage, but there are always exceptions."

"Why do you take them to the police station? Isn't that traumatic for the child?"

"Of course it is, Rhett. We are day care—not a 24/7 babysitting service. If people don't come and get their children, then they're charged with abandoning their child. I'll explain it at another time," she said, lowering her voice when a teacher from the toddler group walked out into the hallway. "We group the children according to age."

Rhett peered through the large window on the door. The shades were drawn and the lights were out. He saw eight tiny bodies on sheet-covered cots under lightweight blankets. "How old are these little munchkins?"

"Those are our two- and three-year-olds. They're all potty-trained, they can feed themselves and all or most recognize the letters in the alphabet. By their third birthday they know their names and addresses, and some can recite their telephone number."

"Do you teach them to read?"

Denise stared at Rhett's profile as he continued to stare into the room. "I've set up a reading-readiness program for the three- and four-year-olds. Some schools are doing away with their pre-K programs, so we've had to pick up the slack. Child care is basically about socialization, but I've tried to incorporate as much education as I can to give our children a head start. When they leave here and enroll in regular school, all are familiar with the alphabet and most of them are able to read.

"The social worker has made it her personal mission to connect with each parent and guardian. If certain deficits are identified, then Tonya becomes a parent's worst nightmare. She will haunt the woman until she either has the child tested or receives the appropriate counseling."

Rhett listened intently when Denise talked about trying to make a difference, not only in the lives of the children but also their families. The center hosted a bimonthly family night for the parents, guardians and siblings of the children. The gatherings served to support the adage that it takes a village to raise a child.

In keeping with the needs of working parents, New Visions had instituted a wellness clinic where children with colds and low-grades fevers were isolated and treated by a nurse practitioner. The children recovered quicker than they would have at home, and their parents didn't have to miss work and stay home with them.

The center was set up to enroll children from six months to twelve years of age. Some school-age children were dropped off at seven, fed breakfast, then lined up for the buses that would take them to their respective schools.

"I'm currently working on a grant to fund an after-school homework or extra help program for middle- and high-school students."

Rhett stared out at the outdoor recreation area enclosed and protected by a high fence and monitored by cameras. There were the requisite slides, teeter-totters, sandboxes, wading pools and picnic tables and benches. All of the classrooms were spacious, with colorful cutouts pasted on windows, reading and play corners and cubbies where coats and boots were stored during colder weather. He'd smiled when seeing the tiny tables and chairs, unable to remember when he'd been that small.

"How much is the grant?" he asked. Denise quoted a figure and he lifted his eyebrows a fraction when he realized what she wanted was less than he'd paid for his car.

"The homework program wouldn't be run here. I don't want the older children interacting with the younger ones."

Shifting, he turned and stared at Denise. "Where will it be?"

Denise gave Rhett a tender smile. "Hopefully I'll be able to rent the space next door."

Taking his hands from his pockets, Rhett took a step

closer to Denise. "Have you talked to the owner about the space?"

She flashed a sexy moue. "Not yet."

"Why haven't you, Ms. Eaton?"

"First, it all depends on a grant I've been working on, so I don't know if I'm going to get the funding."

"And secondly…"

"Secondly, if I did get the funding, I'm not certain whether the owner would be willing to lease the space to New Visions, or what the rent would be."

"Have you completed your budget?"

Denise shook her head. "No. The accountant will do the budget."

"Do you know when you'll submit the grant?"

She nodded. "I have a June fifteenth deadline for submission, and the winners will be announced September fifteenth."

Rhett reached out to touch her hair, but caught himself in time. He remembered Denise's warning about her employees seeing her in a compromising position. "We'll talk about the rent for the space."

"Don't you mean negotiate?" she said.

Attractive lines fanned out around his eyes when he smiled. "Are you willing to negotiate?"

Crossing her arms under her breasts, Denise nodded. "I am if I can get a good deal."

"What do you consider a good deal, Denise?"

"A dollar a month and…"

"And what?" he asked when her words trailed off.

"And I'll make myself available to you more than just weekends."

Rhett narrowed his eyes. "How available is *available?*"

"I'll be your girlfriend."

"You of all people should know what being my girlfriend entails." Denise nodded. Rhett held out his hand. "You've got yourself a deal."

Denise shook his hand. "Deal," she confirmed.

Rhett winked at her. "When do we start?"

"This weekend. I have to get to Paoli by ten, which means we'll have to get on the road early."

"I'll come by and pick you up at six. That should give us plenty of time to get out of D.C. before the traffic builds up. We can stop along the way and have breakfast."

"Pack a bag, Rhett, because I plan to stay overnight in Philly."

"Where are we staying?" he asked.

"I have a co-op in Penn's Landing."

Eli had reported to Rhett that Denise had a buyer for the property and was expected to close on it in a matter of weeks. He never asked the former law enforcement officer how he'd gotten his information, but paid him well for it.

"Okay. We'll spend the night in Philly, but we're going directly to the Cape from there, so you, too, will have to pack enough for two days."

Denise concluded the tour of the facility, walked Rhett back to the reception area and waited until the front door closed behind him. For the second time within two days she chided herself for falling prey to Rhett's charm and her own vulnerability when it came to New Visions. What he hadn't known was that she would agree to almost anything to keep the day care business she built from scratch viable, and that meant sleeping with the man who'd broken her heart.

## Chapter 5

Denise felt excitement akin to what she'd experienced during the ribbon-cutting ceremony when she and the staff of New Visions posed for photo ops with the mayor and other local dignitaries. Rhett's offer to charge her a dollar a month rent for the adjacent vacant building propelled her to complete the grant sooner rather than later. Not having to pay rent meant she could hire an additional instructor.

The space, half the square feet of the day care center, would be configured into classrooms with teachers providing tutoring services in science, math, English and history. She'd wanted to include another subject—technology, but that meant she would have to purchase computers. Unfortunately, the amount of the grant would not cover the cost for new computers. She had considered going to a computer show and purchasing several older models, but decided the technology module would have to wait.

She came in at six in the morning, and several nights she was still at her desk when the night janitor arrived to clean the center. She'd taken a three-day course on grant writing and the seminar proved invaluable when she had to navigate the waters of endless red tape, giving the bureaucrats exactly what they wanted to read and disseminate.

"Don't tell me you're going to spend the weekend here."

Denise's head popped up. The nurse was standing in the doorway. She'd changed out of her colorful scrubs and into jeans and a tank top. The children loved Miss Randi, and it'd taken redheaded, freckled-faced Miranda Gannon a while before she realized the ones who'd deliberately fallen down used it as a ruse to go to the infirmary because she had Band-Aids with their favorite cartoon characters.

"Bite your tongue. As soon as I finish this paragraph I'm outta here."

Miranda rested her hip against the door frame. "If you're staying in town and not really doing anything, I'd like to invite you to hang out with me and Harper."

Denise chuckled. "You, Harper and your brother?" Miranda nodded. "Look, Randi, I know Brice likes me, but what he doesn't understand is that I can't give him the attention he wants."

"He just wants to date you, Denise."

"The man wants to get married. He sees you with Harper and he wants what you have."

Miranda's blue eyes narrowed. "Is it because he has red hair?"

A shiver of annoyance worked its way down Denise's

back. She'd made it a policy not to socialize with her employees, but that was overlooked whenever they hosted a fundraiser or open house. During the last bake sale her parents had surprised her when Paulette donated a dozen cakes and twenty pounds of her prize-winning double chocolate chip cookies.

"Call it for what it is, Miranda. If you're skirting around the issue that I don't want to go out with your brother because he's white, then you're dead wrong. FYI—the last man I dated was white, so there goes your theory as to why I won't date Brice. Now, go home and enjoy your gorgeous husband."

A flush crept up Miranda's neck to her hairline. "I'm sorry, Denise. I had no idea you'd dated out of your race. FYI—I'm going to spend the weekend seeing if Harper and I can make a little brown baby with red hair." She held up a hand. "And, before you get your nose out of joint about losing a nurse, I know someone who will fill in for me while I'm out on maternity leave. Then when Harper or Randi Jr. turns six months he or she will become a New Visions baby."

Denise knew she couldn't remain angry with the perky, kind-hearted nurse. The redhead who'd worked at the Walter Reed Medical Center met and married a psychiatrist decided their marriage would lose its newness if they saw each other 24/7. She applied to the center with impeccable recommendations and after a background check she was hired as the medical director.

"Have fun, Randi."

Miranda winked at Denise. "I intend to. Enjoy your weekend."

"I intend to," Denise repeated.

As soon as she finished up at the center, she planned

to go home and pack for the weekend. Then she would do what she hadn't done in weeks: pick up dinner from her favorite takeout, eat in front of the television, and then take a long relaxing bubble bath before going to bed.

She was looking forward to Belinda's baby shower. Her cousin was listed with several baby registries, and Denise had chosen a number of items and had them shipped to her parents' address. Boaz and Paulette would bring everything to Paoli in their SUV.

Her gaze shifted to the bouquet of flowers on the edge of her desk. Rhett had sent her the flowers as a thank-you gift for sharing dinner with him at the hotel. When she'd called his cell to thank him it went directly to voice mail. That was three days ago.

Her telephone rang and Denise stared at the phone. The display indicated it was a private call. The center was closed; all of the children had been picked up so she couldn't understand who was calling at that hour. After half a dozen rings, the voice mail feature was activated. Less than a minute later her private line rang, and she answered it.

"New Visions Childcare. Denise Eaton speaking."

"Hey."

Denise smiled. "Hey yourself, Rhett. Was it you that just called the main number?"

"Guilty as charged. What are you still doing there?"

"I wanted to finish the grant before I go home."

"Put it away, Denise."

"What?"

"I said put it away and come outside."

"Where are you, Rhett?"

"I'm in the parking lot across the street, leaning

against the bumper of your car. By the way, when did you start driving a hoopty?"

Heat and embarrassment stung her cheeks. "For your information I intend to buy a new car."

"When?"

"That's none of your business."

"I can't believe you were going to drive…*this* to Philly and back."

"Careful, Rhett. You're talking about Valentina."

"Who's Valentina?"

"My *hoopty,* Garrett Mason Fennell. I picked her up on Valentine's Day, so I named her Valentina."

"Tell me something, Denise Amaris Eaton?"

"What is it, Garrett?"

"Why do women name their cars? It's not as if they are pets."

"You wouldn't understand, Rhett. It's a woman thing. Rhett, are you still there?" Denise asked when there came a prolonged pause.

"I'm here. I know it's very short notice, but I'd like to take you out to dinner."

Denise groaned inwardly. "I'd planned to pick up takeout, then go home and have a relaxing bubble bath."

"You can still do that. I'll drop you off home where you can pack—that is if you haven't—then come back to the hotel and order in. After that you can relax in the Jacuzzi until you turn into a raisin."

"What happens after I turn into a raisin?" Her heart was pounding so hard it hurt her chest.

"I'll tuck you into bed, give you a night-night kiss and wait until you fall asleep. Only then will I turn off the light."

Denise remembered how much Rhett liked watching

her until she fell asleep. Only then would he turn off the lamp on his side of the bed. She'd promised to be his girlfriend for the summer, but what she didn't want was for them to pretend all was well and they could pick up where they'd left off what now seemed so long ago.

"Not tonight, Rhett. Maybe some other time."

"I'll see you tomorrow morning."

The phone line went dead and Denise knew he'd hung up. The pain in her chest wasn't because of the runaway beating of her heart. It was heartache, heartache for a man she couldn't trust and for a man she still loved.

It took a quarter of an hour to complete the information needed on the last page of the grant. Denise saved what she'd typed, printed out the pages, then stored everything in a file cabinet and locked it. When she finally walked out of the center after activating the security system, she glanced across the street to see if she could see Rhett. Her car was there, but he was gone.

In less than ten hours she would see Rhett again, and at that time the charade would begin.

Denise walked out of her apartment building carrying a leather tote and a large quilted overnight bag. She wasn't certain whether the gathering she and Rhett were invited to was casual or formal, so she packed outfits for both. Fortunately, the weather had cooperated. Meteorologists predicted sun and warm temperatures for the entire three-day weekend. It was six in the morning and the mercury was already seventy-four degrees.

Less than a minute later a silver Mercedes Benz maneuvered up along the curb and Rhett stepped out. He was casually dressed in a pair of navy linen slacks, a white short-sleeved shirt and black woven slip-ons.

She smiled when he closed the distance between them and reached for her bag. "Good morning."

Rhett angled his head and brushed a kiss over her mouth. "Good morning, beautiful."

She blushed, grateful that her darker coloring hid the heat suffusing her face. It was the same greeting he'd whispered to her whenever they'd slept together. Not only did he look good, but he also smelled good. The cologne was the perfect complement for his personality. It was masculine, yet subtle.

"I'll keep the tote," she said when he reached for that, too.

"What's in there?"

"My wallet with my driver's license and a few feminine incidentals."

"Are you going to need your tampons and sanitary napkins before we get to Philly?"

"No, he didn't ask me that," she said under her breath.

"Yes, I did," Rhett countered, taking the tote from her loose grip, shifting both bags to one hand, while the other cupped her elbow. "I was the only guy at Johns Hopkins who bought his girlfriend's tampons and pads. The wise-ass in checkout once asked me if I'd had a sex change."

Smiling, Denise gave him a sidelong glance. "You never told me that."

Rhett helped her into the passenger seat, stored the bags in the trunk, then came around and slid behind the wheel. "That's because I was too embarrassed to repeat it."

Denise buckled her seat belt. "Well, I bought our condoms."

Shifting into gear, he pulled away from the curb.

"Lots of girls buy condoms, because they don't trust guys not to put holes in them with pins or needles."

"That's not why I bought the condoms, Rhett. Neither of us wanted nor needed a baby at that time in our lives."

"What about now? Are you ready to start a family?"

Staring out the windshield, Denise pondered his query. It was one she'd asked herself every time she celebrated a birthday. She would celebrate her twenty-eighth birthday at the end of September and each year brought her closer to when she would be deemed high-risk.

She loved children and eventually wanted to become a mother but didn't want to be a baby mama. More than half the women who'd enrolled their children in New Visions were single mothers, most struggling to make ends meet. Even those who had earned a college degree and were making fairly good salaries had to monitor their budgets closely because it was becoming more and more difficult to support a family of two, three or even four on one salary.

"No," Denise said after a swollen silence. "I still have a few years to think about it."

"Don't think too long, sweetheart."

She turned to look at Rhett, silently admiring his distinctive profile. He held his head at a slight angle that she'd always found very endearing. "Why would you say that?"

"I remember you saying you didn't want to be faced with the countdown of a ticking biological clock."

"I still have a few years before the clock starts ticking. What about you, Rhett? Are you ready to become a daddy?"

"Yeah, I believe I am. Business is good despite

the soft real estate market. If I had any doubts before about fatherhood they were dashed once I saw the little darlings at your center."

"They are precious," Denise said proudly. "I'd like you to join us when we host our welcome summer party. We've made it a tradition to throw a party for each season where we celebrate all the holidays that fall within that season. The kids love the summer celebration because we grill outdoors and they get to splash around in the wading pools."

Rhett followed the signs leading to the interstate. "It looks as if we made our dreams come true."

Denise smiled. "We talked about what we wanted enough, so all that was left was putting it into action. You wanted to run your own business and I wanted a career in education."

"How long did you remain in the classroom?" He was asking a question to which he knew the answer.

"Four years."

"Four years as a classroom teacher, two years as the director of one of the most progressive child care facilities in the Capitol district and you plan to set up an after-school homework/tutoring program for middle- and high-school students. That's quite an accomplishment, and all before you celebrate your thirtieth birthday. Speaking of the big three-oh, I submitted your name to the editor for the *Beltway Business Review* thirty under thirty rising star. Don't be surprised if you get a call to submit some paperwork for the thirty under thirty awards."

Denise's jaw dropped. "No, you didn't."

"Yes, I did, Denise. Don't be so modest. You deserve the recognition."

"I do what I do because I love it, not because I need validation from a group of businesspeople."

"It's not about validation, baby. It's about you setting an example for those who will come behind you, and because you did it some young girl will believe that she can do it, too. You're blessed, because you have a family of educators as your role model.

"I had no male figures in my life when growing up. I didn't know my father, my grandfather was dead and my aunts were either widowed or single. If my mother hadn't scrimped and saved to send me to a boarding school where I was mentored by their only male black teacher I don't know where I'd be now.

"Although teachers were forbidden to interact with students if it didn't pertain to education, Mr. Evans used the ruse that he was tutoring me whenever we met in the school library. He was a parole officer—a clergyman, psychologist and teacher rolled into one brilliant man who'd spent most of his life in foster care after his father murdered his mother. He taught me to use what God had given all of us—my brain. I was told I was smart, but I hadn't realized how smart until I competed with the other boys whose parents were graduates of elite finishing schools and Ivy League colleges.

"What really saved me in going to an all-boy boarding school is that I wasn't distracted by girls. It was hard as hell to study for a chemistry exam when my hormones were short-circuiting. It took a while for me to catch on that some of the upperclassmen, instead of going home on the weekends, would hang around campus, then pile into taxis and go to a little town where women charged the students for sex. Most of the boys had money to burn, so they literally screwed their brains out. My mother sent me money for what she called my emergency fund."

"And for you, sex was an emergency," Denise said, smiling.

"It'd become a welcome respite from living with two hundred boys 24/7."

Denise found it odd that Rhett had never talked much about his boarding school experience before. The only thing he'd told her was that his mother had sent him to a private school in northern Virginia to ensure he wouldn't be tempted to join a gang that was recruiting boys with the promise of drugs, guns and girls.

"Had your mother known you were sexually active?"

Rhett waited for a passing car, then accelerated into fast-moving traffic heading north. "She found out after she discovered a condom I'd left in the pocket of my uniform slacks. She'd put it on my bed with a note that we had to talk when she got back from work. I was surprised when she didn't go into a rant, because at sixteen she felt I was too young to engage in sexual relations with a woman, but commended me that I'd taken the precaution to practice safe sex. What bothered her was the possibility of my becoming a teenage father. I'd promised her I wouldn't father a child until I married. I knew what she'd had to go through as a single mother and I didn't want the same for my child or children."

Denise didn't want to tell Rhett that he sounded like a public announcement sound bite only because she knew how careful he'd been not to get her pregnant. They'd gone from using condoms to her eventually taking an oral contraceptive. Too often young coeds, away from home for the first time, found themselves pregnant in their freshman year. A few had abortions while some dropped out to have their babies.

Their conversation segued from sex and parenthood to innocuous topics ranging from television shows, movies and celebrity gossip. They'd lapsed into the smooth and uncomplicated camaraderie they'd shared before infidelity and distrust shattered their world and future.

Closing her eyes and settling back on the leather seat, Denise smiled. The sound of soft jazz coming from the vehicle's powerful sound system was incredible. Luxury seating, a navigation system and a surround sound audio system caressed her senses. "How long have you had this car?"

"I picked it up in January. Why?"

"It still has that new-car smell."

"It's my first new car," Rhett admitted.

Denise opened her eyes, giving him an incredulous look. She didn't know his net worth, but it was reported that he'd become a millionaire before he'd turned twenty-six. "What did you drive?"

"Used cars. The first two definitely were hoopty status. I lost a tailpipe on the parkway and I thought the car was going to explode because the pipe left a trail of sparks that made it look as if the car was about to take off. Another needed a catalytic converter and it made so much noise that it set off car alarms whenever I drove past. I managed to upgrade every year, but they were still used. Last year, I decided it was time to step up and treat myself to something new."

"You stepped up nicely."

"Thank you. Let me know when you're going to replace Valentina and I'll go with you. Some salesmen tend to take advantage of women whenever they go to purchase a car."

"I'm going to wait until the fall when the new models come out before I make a decision."

"I'll still go with you," Rhett insisted. The sign indicating the number of miles to Philadelphia came into view. "I'm going to stop so we can eat."

Denise glanced at the clock on the dashboard. It was after seven. It'd taken an hour to go forty miles. Holiday traffic was heavy and slow-moving.

"Okay."

She wanted to tell Rhett that she didn't want to linger too long because she and Chandra would have a small window of time in which to decorate the house before Griffin and Belinda returned to Paoli.

Rhett maneuvered into an empty space in the parking lot of a restaurant off the interstate offering family-style dining. Leaning to his right, he pressed a kiss to Denise's temple. "Don't worry, baby, we'll get there in plenty of time."

She nodded. He'd read her mind.

# Chapter 6

When Denise directed Rhett down the tree-lined street in Paoli to the house where Griffin and Belinda lived with their twin nieces, she'd tried to ignore the flutters in her belly. It was as if she'd come full circle. Instead of bringing Garrett Fennell with her to meet her parents, he was accompanying her to a gathering where most Eatons were expected to attend.

She didn't want to send the wrong message, but with Rhett in tow everyone would assume they'd reconciled and now were a couple. And she was certain it would be easier for Rhett because he'd lapsed into calling her *sweetheart* and *baby* as if they'd had an ongoing relationship.

"There's Chandra's car." She pointed to the dark blue sports car parked at the end of the block.

"Where do you want me to park?" Rhett asked.

"Pull up behind her Audi. If we park in the driveway, then Belinda's going to know something's up."

He followed her instructions, parking and cutting off the engine. She waited for him to get out and come around to assist her. With the exception of the men in her family, Rhett was the only man who'd exhibited impeccable manners. He opened and closed car doors, held doors open for her, seated her in restaurants and stood up whenever a woman entered the room. He claimed it was something that had been drilled into him at the boarding school.

Rhett retrieved Denise's leather tote, carrying it while he escorted her across the street to the three-story Colonial set on a half-acre lot. Although he'd visited Philadelphia, he'd never ventured into the suburbs. Large nineteenth-century homes set on expansive lawns and massive century-old trees projected a postcard perfect picture where people could live and raise a family in exclusive comfort.

"This is very nice," he said softly.

"I love this place," Denise confirmed. "There was a time when anyone living in Paoli was identified as the *crème de la crème* of Philadelphia society."

"It still looks that way to me. After all, Griffin Rice is as much a celebrity as the clients he represents."

There had been a time when the high-profile sports attorney had been a favorite of the paparazzi when they snapped pictures of him with his famous clients, glamorous models, beautiful actresses and recording stars. But his electrifying lifestyle changed when his brother and sister-in-law were killed in a horrific car accident and as a legal guardian along with Belinda Eaton had become the parents of their twin nieces.

Griffin settled smoothly into the role as stepfather,

and after he married Belinda had become husband *and* father. Now, he and Belinda were expecting their first child. Tests confirmed it was a boy.

Denise led Rhett around to the rear of the house. She smiled when she saw Preston Tucker removing folding chairs from a rack and setting them up under two long rectangular tables.

She hugged and kissed the brilliant, award-winning playwright. "Hey, P.J. I'm glad something pulled you away from your computer."

Easing back, she met a pair of sensual, slanting heavy-lidded eyes that were mesmerizing. There was more gray in his cropped hair than had been when she saw him at Christmas. There was no doubt Preston would be completely gray before his fortieth birthday. She'd been maid of honor at Preston and Chandra's Thanksgiving Isle of Palms wedding.

Preston Tucker chuckled softly. "Chandra would've had a hissy fit if I didn't come."

Denise held out her hand to Rhett, he taking it and threading their fingers together. "Preston, this is my very good friend, Garrett Fennell. Rhett, this is my cousin Preston Tucker."

Rhett, who'd set Denise's tote on a chair, extended his free hand. "My pleasure, Preston. Denise didn't tell me she was related to P.J. Tucker."

"I married her cousin last fall."

"Congratulations. Are you working on something new?" he asked the playwright.

"I just finished editing a new play in which I'd collaborated with my very talented wife." As if on cue, Chandra walked out the house carrying a box. Preston raced over and took it from her. "I told you not to carry anything."

Chandra sucked her teeth loudly, a habit that annoyed her mother. "It's filled with paper, Preston."

"I don't care if it's filled with air. I don't want to see you carrying anything."

Denise whistled sharply through her teeth. It'd taken her more than a week of coaching from her brother before she was able to make the piercing sound. "Will someone please tell me what's going on here?"

Preston glared at Chandra. "She's pregnant, and the doctor cautioned her about heavy lifting."

Denise did the happy dance, spinning around like a whirling dervish. "You didn't tell me you were going to have a baby," she shrieked, hugging her cousin around her neck.

Chandra Eaton-Tucker pushed her back. "Please don't get too close. Every time I smell perfume or cologne I hurl."

"How far along are you?" Denise asked, taking a backward step.

"Just six weeks."

She turned to Rhett. "I don't think I have to introduce you two."

Rhett smiled at the woman who looked enough like Denise to be her sister. They had the same almond-shaped eyes, high cheekbones, pert nose and lush mouth. The first cousins both had curly hair, but Chandra had always affected a wild flyaway style that suited her free-spirited personality, while Denise's shorter style was more conservative. Mrs. Tucker had tamed her curls by pulling them into a single braid.

Chandra blew Rhett an air kiss. "I would hug you, but I know you're wearing cologne. You have no idea how good it is to see you again, Rhett."

"That goes double for me, Chandra. Congratulations on your marriage *and* the baby."

Chandra moved closer to Preston, looping her arm through his. "Thank you. I hope you don't let my cousin run away again now that you're aware that she's a flight risk."

Denise made a cutting motion over her throat. "Chandra!"

"Denise!" Chandra mimicked. "Well, it's true."

Preston dropped a kiss on his wife's hair. "Get out of their business, baby," he said softly. "Please, baby," he added when she opened her mouth to come back at him.

Rhett gave Preston a surreptitious nod, discernible only to the two men. "What do you want Denise and me to help you with?"

"You can finish setting up the chairs while I fill the pool."

Denise mouthed a thank-you to Rhett as she took the box filled with party favors and streamers from Preston. "Chandra, I want you to sit while I decorate."

"I'm pregnant, not an invalid," Chandra mumbled.

"Go sit down and don't talk back," Denise said firmly.

"Like damn, cousin. You don't have to get so *hoss-tile.*"

Denise waved her hand in dismissal. "Preston, please handle your wife. Rhett and I will do what needs to be done."

Chandra pulled away from Preston, sitting down in a huff, while crossing her arms under her breasts. Preston brought over a footstool and placed her feet on the cushion, then removed her sandals. Leaning down, he kissed her mouth. "Relax, baby."

It took less than an hour for them to set up the chairs, cover the tables with kiwi-green and chocolate tablecloths and fill the inground pool. It took several tries before Preston was able to get the chlorine to a safe level. Rhett checked the tanks of propane and then hooked them to the gas grills. The men set up the tent, attaching streamers of brown and green to the poles. Deliveries of balloons, bouquets of flowers and potted flowering plants added a festive touch to the outdoor space.

Myles, his wife, Zabrina, and their son, Adam, were the first to arrive. The day before they'd driven from Pittsburgh to Philadelphia, checking into a downtown hotel for the night.

If Myles seemed surprised to see Rhett, he didn't show it when he pulled him close in a rough hug. "Don't be like me, brother. I had to wait ten years before I got my woman back."

Denise hugged Adam. "If you don't stop growing you're going to be taller than me in a couple of years," she teased, kissing his cheek.

Curly-haired, golden-eyed Adam Eaton gave her a shy smile. "The doctor said I'm going to be taller than my dad."

Denise smiled at the eleven-year-old. He'd inherited his mother's hair and eyes, but his lanky frame was his father's. "That's the way it usually goes. Each generation is usually taller than the one before it."

"Even girls?"

She nodded. "Even girls."

"So, if Mom has a girl she'll be taller than her?"

Peering over Adam's shoulder, Denise saw what hadn't been obvious from first glance. Zabrina's face was fuller, and her breasts under a loose-fitting top also appeared larger.

She smiled. The Eatons were about to have a population explosion. First Belinda, Chandra and probably Zabrina. Dr. Dwight and Roberta Eaton would have back-to-back-to-back grandchildren.

"Yes, Adam. Chances are she would be taller than your mother."

She didn't want to ask him if his mother was pregnant, and if she was, then Zabrina and Myles would probably make the announcement after the shower was over, or perhaps even at another time.

Eatons were arriving by the carloads, all bearing gaily-wrapped gifts. It'd been a while since Denise had seen her uncles and their wives. Her great-grandfather came to Philadelphia as a young boy during the Great Migration. Daniel Eaton had worked two jobs all his life to give his children what had eluded him: a college education. Her grandfather, Daniel Eaton Jr., earned a law degree from Howard University and three of his five sons followed in his footsteps, while the other two became physicians. The five brothers married schoolteachers, establishing the criteria for future generations to select careers in law, medicine or education.

Denise waved to her parents as they joined the others on the patio where the noise level had increased exponentially as relatives greeted one another with laughter and excited shrieks. Xavier followed Boaz and Paulette, carrying boxes she knew were filled with her mother's incredible cake creations.

Weaving her way through the crowd, she looped her arms around her mother's waist. Paulette Eaton had put on a little weight since she'd retired. "Hi, Mom."

Paulette kissed her daughter's cheek. "I heard you and Rhett were back together," she said quietly.

Denise smiled at her mother who'd been a Temple University homecoming queen and was still stunning at fifty-six. Her flawless sable-brown skin, large dark eyes and fashionably cut black hair still turned heads. "We just started seeing each other again. We decided to hang out together for the summer, then see where it goes."

Paulette narrowed her eyes. "You let him get away once. Don't be *no* fool, Denise Amaris Eaton," she drawled. "Not many women are blessed enough to get a second chance with the man they love. And I still don't believe your excuse that you'd fallen out of love with Garrett. Remember, I'm your mother and I know you better than you think I do. You're still in love with him and he's still in love with you. So, stop the foolishness, marry the man and give me a grandchild. I can't stand Roberta now that Belinda's about to give her another grandbaby. She's struttin' around with her nose so far up in the air that if it rained she'd drown."

Denise gasped, complete shock freezing her features. For a reason she couldn't fathom, her mother had always competed with Chandra's mother. Roberta and Dwight had had four children to Paulette's two and all of Roberta's children were married and either had, or would give her grandchildren, while Paulette was waiting for her first.

"Mama, what has Aunt Bertie ever done to you where you have to bad-mouth her?"

"She couldn't wait to call me and gloat when Belinda told her she was having a baby. It was the same when Donna had the twins. Then when she found out that Myles had a son that took the rag off the bush." Paulette's eyes filled with tears. "She knows how much I want a grandchild."

"What if you never have grandchildren? What then? And I shouldn't have to remind you that you *do* have a son."

"Harrumph!" Paulette snorted. "I'd probably be old as Methuselah by the time Xavier decides to settle down with a woman long enough to marry and start a family." She snorted again, squared her shoulders and walked across the patio, heading straight for Rhett.

Denise smothered a curse. Whenever her mother embarked on a campaign it was always advisable to stay out of her way.

"I've been reading some good things about you, son," Boaz Eaton said to Rhett, while pumping his hand vigorously. "Congratulations."

Rhett smiled. "Thank you, Judge."

Boaz wagged a finger. "None of that judge business, Rhett. I'm not sitting on the bench, or wearing a black robe. I don't know why you and my daughter broke up, and I don't want to know why. But I must say it is nice to see you together again. I never much cared for that other fellow she dated a couple of years ago, but I'm not one to get into my children's personal business, so when she finally gave him his walking papers I was as happy as a pig in slop."

Rhett realized Denise's father had revealed something that hadn't been in Eli Oakes's report. She had been involved with another man, and he knew for certain the man wasn't Trey Chambers. But for some unknown and perverted sense of jealousy it bothered him that she had been with a man when he was hard-pressed to remember all of the women he'd had after they'd separated.

Rhett wanted to tell the older man that he and Denise were together not because they had fallen in love again, but because of his need for revenge. His love for Denise Eaton had defied description, yet she'd fallen prey to lies fabricated by Trey Chambers. It wouldn't have mattered if she'd believed the lies, but sleeping with Trey had been the ultimate betrayal.

He smiled at the man who should've become his father-in-law. Boaz Eaton reminded Rhett of the elegant-looking black men in the photographs taken by James Van Der Zee. He was tall, slender and the rimless glasses added to his overall patrician appearance.

"Denise and I are giving ourselves the summer to see if we can make it work this time," Rhett said instead.

Boaz leaned in closer. "My daughter is a great deal like her mother. She tends to be a little difficult at times. But don't let up on her, son. If she's worth having, then she's worth fighting for."

"I'll keep that in mind."

At one time Denise had been worth fighting for, but Rhett hadn't had the wherewithal to fight the fight. He had been a month from graduating, he had a position waiting for him at a major real estate company with perks that included tuition reimbursement for graduate studies. Instead of fighting for Denise, he'd walked away.

"Welcome back, stranger."

Rhett turned when he heard the familiar voice belonging to Xavier Eaton. The two men exchanged handshakes. "Thanks. What's up?"

Xavier's dark eyes took in everything about the man who'd at one time been the love of his sister's life. "Not much. Did Denise tell you I left the military on a medical discharge?"

"Yes, she did happen to mention it."

"I was in a funk and wallowing in pity parties until my sister forced me to see that my life wasn't over, that I could remain involved with the military if I taught. I applied to several military schools and colleges and come September I'll begin teaching a few courses on military history at a school in South Carolina. I—"

"Xavier, could you please help your father bring in the gifts from the car, while I talk to Garrett?"

"Good luck," Xavier whispered under his breath as he walked away.

Rhett stepped forward, lowered his head and kissed Paulette Eaton's cheek. "How are you?"

Reaching up, Paulette patted his clean-shaven jaw. "I'm just fine, Garrett. My, my, my, you look wonderful."

"Thank you, Mrs. Eaton."

Paulette's dark eyes sparkled like polished jet. "How is your mother doing?"

"She married a wonderful man last year, and they're now living in Virginia."

"She was always such a lovely woman. When you talk to her, please let her know I asked about her."

Rhett smiled. "I will."

"Now that you and my daughter are together again, can I look forward to planning a wedding?"

"No, you can't, Mom."

Denise had come up behind her mother just in time to hear her ask Rhett a question that made her want to scream at Paulette for the first time in her life.

Paulette gave Denise a too-sweet smile. "If Garrett is able to negotiate multimillion-dollar deals, then I believe he's capable of answering for himself."

Rhett wanted to tell Paulette he'd just negotiated

a deal with her daughter based on revenge, but she'd flipped the script when she invited him to come with her to a family gathering where everyone expected them to pick up as if six years hadn't happened. As if their beautiful, talented Denise hadn't slept with his best friend while professing her love for him.

"I'd say planning a wedding is a little premature at this time. Denise and I have just begun dating again, so we've decided to keep our options open about the future."

"What options are you talking about?" Paulette asked.

"Mom, please," Denise pleaded.

"Don't…" A loud roar filled the air, stopping what would become a rant from Paulette.

A very pregnant Belinda Rice, supported by her husband, had covered her face when she saw the decorations and the small crowd that had gathered on the patio of her home.

Her hand came down as she cradled her belly with both hands. "It would serve y'all right if I drop this baby right now." She glared at Griffin Rice. "You had to be in on this. Riding my behind up and down the road when you know I have to have bathroom breaks every twenty minutes."

Denise reached for Rhett's hand, lacing their fingers together. It was as if they'd turned back the clock and holding hands was as natural to them as breathing.

"For a woman who is expected to deliver any day, Belinda looks so incredibly beautiful," she whispered to Rhett. Belinda had cut her hair and the scooped-neck white tunic over a pair of black cropped pants artfully concealed her swollen belly.

"She does," he confirmed.

Belinda was more attractive than Rhett had remembered, but so was Denise. He'd barely touched her, except to hold hands, had kissed her once and not with the passion racing headlong throughout his body whenever they shared the same space, and yet he wanted her with a ferocity that overshadowed everything that had happened between them.

Denise was right when she'd reminded him of his revelation that he'd felt more connected to her than he had with any other woman. The monies he'd paid to the nameless, faceless women—his mother's hard-earned money—for sex had been nothing more than a receptacle for his lust. The women he'd slept with after he and Denise split up he paid in other ways: dinners, gifts and exotic vacations. Despite the moans, groans and unorthodox positions, none of them had touched the part of him he'd withheld from every woman except Denise Eaton.

Initially Rhett had believed he'd stayed with her out of guilt because he'd taken her virginity. But when he finally recognized that what he'd felt for Denise was an unconditional love that would stand the test of time, he knew he'd made the right decision to continue to see her.

Rhett closed his eyes for several seconds. He'd lured Denise into a trap to assuage a vendetta—something he should have dealt with six years ago. Her family believed they'd reconciled when what they had was a business arrangement. She'd gone along with his scheme to save and expand her business, while he'd sought to take advantage of her vulnerability.

If his mother were to uncover what he'd done, Rhett knew she would disown him. Once he'd told Geraldine that he was going to set up his own company she'd warned him about storing up material wealth at the risk of losing his soul. "Please don't end up like your father." When he'd asked her what she meant, Geraldine ordered him to leave her alone. It had been the first and last time his mother had spoken of his father.

He had made a lot of money buying out failing companies, stabilizing and then flipping them, but not at the risk of losing his soul—until now. Manipulating and blackmailing Denise made him no better than the man who'd fathered him. A man his mother was loathe to speak of. A man whose name she'd never uttered in his presence.

Rhett gave Denise's hand a gentle squeeze. He smiled, meeting her questioning gaze. "Thank you for asking me to come with you today. It's been a long time since I've felt a part of a family unit."

"That's because the Eatons have always thought of you as family, Rhett."

"What about you, Denise? Can you think of me as family?"

A beat passed. "Where are you going with this, Rhett?"

"I want you to forget everything we talked about at the hotel."

"Come with me," Denise ordered, pulling away from the others to a corner of the patio where they wouldn't be overheard. "Talk to me, Rhett."

Releasing her hand, he cradled her face gently between his palms. "I'm releasing you from our agreement. I won't double your rent, and when your lease renewal comes due it will be no more than five percent. And… and you don't have to stand in as my hostess if you don't want to."

Denise blinked. "I don't understand. What brought on this change of heart?"

Rhett wanted to tell Denise he wanted what Belinda had with Griffin, what Myles had with Zabrina and what Chandra had with Preston. He wanted to marry the woman with whom he'd fallen in love with years ago, and still loved.

"The day care center," he said cryptically.

"What about New Visions?"

"It's about you providing quality child care for the people who need it most. It's about you making sacrifices in your personal life to make a difference for those less fortunate. I realized that last night when I tried to lure you away from your work to have dinner with me. Unfortunately, I let my ego get in the way of common sense."

Denise covered his hands with hers. She'd never known Rhett to be self-deprecating, and she felt no joy in seeing him humbled. "Thank you for not increasing the rent where it would become fiscally impossible to keep the doors open." Going on tiptoe, she pressed her mouth to his. "I've heard that all work and no play can make one quite dull. If you can assure me that we'll have fun this summer then I'm more than willing to stand in as your date and hostess."

Rhett's smile reached his eyes, making them dance with delight. "I promise that you'll have the time of your life."

## Chapter 7

A bartender had arrived and was busy mixing drinks for the assembly, while the caterer and his staff had set up trays of prepared foods at the far end of the patio. Twin grills were fired up to offer grill-to-order steaks, burgers and the perennial hot dogs.

Adam and his twin cousins, Sabrina and Layla, had changed into swimwear and preferred playing in the pool to eating. Chandra, who'd taken the responsibility for coordinating her sister's baby shower, wanted everyone to eat and drink before Belinda opened her gifts.

It was as if a permanent smile was pasted on Griffin Rice's incredibly handsome face. He'd become the consummate host, seeing to the needs of the respective grandparents Dr. Dwight and Roberta Eaton and Lucas and Gloria Rice.

Denise sat at the table between Rhett and Preston Tucker. She saw her mother's gaze on her whenever she leaned closer to Rhett to hear what he was saying to her. Each time their shoulders touched she felt a jolt of awareness race through her to settle in the region between her legs.

He'd offered her an out but instead of running as fast as she could in the opposite direction, she'd elected to spend the summer with him to see if she could recapture some of the magic from their past. If they continued to see each other beyond the summer then she would enjoy it, but if they didn't then she would know it wasn't meant to be.

Her life had become so predictable that if anyone wanted to stalk her it would be very easy for them to monitor her whereabouts. Denise went from her apartment to the center, then back again. The only time her day deviated was when she attended board meetings on the two organizations where she'd become a member.

She'd made it a practice not to socialize with her staff except when it was necessary. At twenty-eight she was younger than most of the staff, and Denise didn't want to compromise her authority by becoming too familiar with them. Age aside, it had been her hard work and a business loan that provided them with the means of collecting a biweekly paycheck.

She swallowed the last of a delicious concoction filled with fruit slices and liberally laced with rum. It tasted like Hi-C, but the effects were lethal. Closing her eyes, she rested her head on Rhett's shoulder.

"I feel as if I'm swimming in the Bermuda Triangle."

Cradling her hand under the table, Rhett dropped a kiss on her hair. "Poor baby can't hang out with the grown folks," he teased.

"You know I can't drink."

"That's okay, baby. I'll be your designated driver."

She opened her eyes and smiled at him. "I think I like you, Rhett Fennell."

"You think?"

"Okay. I know I like you."

Rhett wanted to tell Denise that he more than liked her. He was in love with her. "Do you want to go inside and lie down?"

She shook her head. "No. I'm good. It's just that I have to wait until my head stops spinning."

Rhett looked at her plate. She'd barely touched her food. Releasing her hand, he picked up her fork and speared a forkful of potato salad. "Open your mouth, darling."

Denise complied and over the next ten minutes she permitted Rhett to feed her, unaware of those at the table throwing surreptitious glances their way. The fuzziness in her head subsided and she took the fork from Rhett and cleaned her plate.

There was another flurry of activity when chairs were adjusted to accommodate another one of Daniel's sons, who'd come in from Texas with his daughter instead of his wife, who was recovering from eye surgery and had been cautioned not to fly. Dr. Hyman Eaton went around the table kissing everyone while his daughter, Mia, a fourth-year medical student, hugged and kissed Belinda before resting a hand over her distended belly.

"It's incredible that your father and his brothers all look alike," Rhett said in Denise's ear.

The fourth Eaton brother, Solomon, a Dade County federal prosecutor, had flown up for the day, but was scheduled to take a red-eye back to Florida later that night because he was awaiting the decision on an extortion and racketeering case that had become front-page news.

"They look like their father. The exception is Raleigh, who's laid up with a broken foot. He looks like my grandmother. My dad and his brothers used to tease him, saying they found him on the doorstep and decided to keep him. His comeback is that he's the only good-looking one among the bunch, so he knows he's special. Uncle Raleigh happens to be the only one who can't seem to make a go of his marriages. I think he's now on his fourth wife."

"Damn!" Rhett whispered.

"Ditto," Denise said, laughing softly.

The sun had passed its zenith when Griffin Rice, sitting beside his pregnant wife, handed her gaily-wrapped gifts as she read the attached cards aloud before carefully and methodically removing the paper. The gifts ranged from a changing table, crib mobiles, cartons of disposable diapers, wipes, several bottle sterilizers, countless packages of socks, undershirts in varying sizes, bibs, sweaters, hats, baby monitors, crib sheets and blankets, towels and grooming supplies and a table lamp. The grandparents had shared the cost of purchasing the nursery furniture.

Denise had paid the grandmother of one of the center's children to hand-quilt a blanket in differing shades of green and brown—the colors Belinda had chosen for the nursery. The result was a stunning piece of art. She also gave Belinda the complete set of the Little Golden Books for her to read to her son.

"You didn't have to do that," she chided Rhett when Griffin thanked him for the savings bond for the baby's college fund.

Rhett glared at Denise for a full minute. "Don't ever tell me what I can or cannot do with *my* money," he said between clenched teeth.

She recoiled as if he'd struck her across the face. "Well, excuse me."

"You *are* excused, Miss Eaton." He pressed the pad of his thumb to her lips, before he angled his head and kissed her. "Sometime that mouth of yours is going to get you into a world of hurt."

Denise saw her brother out of the corner of her eye as he came closer. He was limping, which meant he was either in pain or tired. She touched his shoulder. "Are you all right, Xavier?"

Silky black eyes flickered slightly. "I'm good. I just came to tell you two to take that face-sucking inside. After all, there are kids here."

"FYI—the kids are in the house playing video games. Don't tell me you're jealous, my favorite brother."

Xavier smiled, revealing beautiful straight white teeth. "A little. I'm glad you guys are back together." He slapped Rhett on the back. "Take care of my sister."

Rhett gave Xavier a level stare. "You don't have to worry about that."

"Just don't make me have to worry," Xavier countered, walking away and leaving them staring at his back.

It didn't take an IQ of genius for Rhett to realize he'd been warned *and* threatened. He wanted to tell the ex-soldier that he hadn't been the one to walk out on his sister. It had been her decision to end their relationship. Denise calling his name recaptured his attention.

"What is it, baby?"

"I said I'm going into the kitchen to help my mother bring out dessert. After that we can leave whenever you want."

Rhett nodded. "Okay.

* * *

The waitstaff had begun putting food away and cleaning up. Meanwhile Belinda had retreated into the house to lie down. Over slices of cake, pie and cupcakes, Preston and Chandra announced they were expecting and the baby was due two months after celebrating their first wedding anniversary. Myles and Zabrina added to the excitement when they revealed they were expecting their second child, a girl, at the end of September. They hadn't said anything earlier because Zabrina had been on bed rest during her first trimester.

Denise refused to look at her mother, who was shooting daggers at Roberta, who wept openly when she realized she would celebrate the birth of three grandchildren in one calendar year.

She leaned in closer to Rhett. "As soon as I say my goodbyes, we can leave." She wasn't going to hang around and be forced to deal with Paulette Eaton's histrionics.

It seemed like an eternity when she hugged and kissed her relatives. After promising Chandra she would call her, she and Rhett were able to make their escape.

Seated and belted-in with the engine running, Rhett stared at the woman seated beside him. "Give me the address of your place." She gave it to him and he programmed it into the navigational system.

They didn't talk during the ride from Paoli to Philadelphia. There was only the sound of music coming from the automobile's powerful speakers to break the comfortable silence.

Denise stepped out of the elevator, Rhett following and carrying their bags, as she led him down the carpeted hallway to her apartment. She was counting down the weeks until she would be free of the responsibility of maintaining the space.

She'd continued to pay the maintenance on the co-op *and* rent on her D.C. apartment, because she hadn't been able to find someone willing to buy it, until Chandra returned from a stint in the Peace Corps and offered to sublet it. Her cousin had barely moved in when a month later she vacated the co-op to live with her husband.

Denise unlocked the door and pushed it open. The scent of pine and lemon wafted in her nostrils. It was obvious the cleaning service had come by to dust and air out rooms that hadn't been occupied in weeks. Whenever she drove to Philly to visit her parents she'd made it a practice to stay in the apartment rather than in the bedroom in the large house where she'd grown up.

Stepping aside, she smiled at Rhett. "Welcome to my humble abode," she drawled, flipping the switch and turning on an overhead Tiffany-style hanging fixture.

Rhett entered the immaculate apartment. The light from the fixture was reflected in the high gloss of the wood floor. He set down the bags in the entryway as Denise closed and locked the door.

He didn't know what to expect, but it wasn't oyster-white walls and a living room with a white seating grouping with differing blue accessories. The living room flowed into a dining area with an oak oval pedestal table with seating for six. To the right of the dining area was a set of four steps that led directly into the kitchen.

Walking across the open space, he peered through wall-to-wall pale silk drapes to look out on the water. The Benjamin Franklin Bridge spanning the Delaware River was clearly visible from the sixth-floor apartment.

Denise joined Rhett at the window, drawing back the drapes. "I love this view, especially at sunset or after a snowfall."

Rhett reached for her hand. "I don't know what your D.C. apartment looks like, but this one is fabulous."

"The one in D.C. is nice, too."

"Why do you have two apartments?" He'd asked the question even though he knew the answer. Eli Oakes's investigative report on Denise Eaton was very comprehensive. What he hadn't uncovered was her relationship with the man Judge Eaton had spoken of. It was apparent her father hadn't approved of the man.

"I own this one, but hopefully not for much longer. I have a June tenth closing date."

"What if you don't close?" he asked.

Denise blew out her cheeks. "Bite your tongue, Rhett. I've been trying to sell this place for nearly two years. Thankfully I don't have a mortgage, so there's just the maintenance fee. When the bottom fell out of the real estate market, banks weren't willing to write mortgages. Some of them were asking for a third down, and for most people that's an impossibility.

"Chandra, who'd spent two years in Belize as a Peace Corps volunteer, returned home last fall, asking to move in. I told her she could stay as long as she wanted. All she had to do was pay the maintenance. However, that lasted about a month. She'd met P.J. Tucker and hadn't planned to marry him until this June, but he didn't want to wait, so they had a Thanksgiving wedding."

"Where do they live?"

"Preston has a condo in a beautiful historic neighborhood known as Rittenhouse and a country house in the Brandywine Valley."

"If you only have to pay the maintenance, why get rid of it, Denise?"

"I can't afford to maintain two residences on my salary."

Rhett squeezed her fingers. "If the deal falls through, I'll buy it from you."

"Do you need another place to live?"

Releasing her hand, he pulled Denise close until she stood between his legs. "No. I'd used it for rental income."

"How are you going to monitor a tenant when you live—"

Rhett kissed Denise, stopping her words *and* her breath. It was what he'd wanted to do the moment he saw her enter the hotel lobby. In that instant everything he'd felt and believed about her since their separation vanished, replaced by a rushing desire for a woman who'd touched him in a way no other had or probably would.

His mouth caressed hers, as he left nibbling kisses at the corners of her mouth, biting gently on her lower lip before giving the upper one equal attention. "Do you know how long I've wanted to taste your mouth?" The admission was drawn from someplace Rhett hadn't known existed.

Curving her arms under his shoulders, Denise pressed closer, the curves of her body fitting into the hard contours of Rhett's body. He'd confessed that he'd wanted to kiss her when she'd wanted the same.

She'd picked at her food when they'd had dinner in The Lafayette, because whenever she'd stared at Rhett's mouth the images of how he'd used his mouth and tongue to bring her maximum pleasure wouldn't permit her to chew and swallow a morsel without choking.

Denise gasped when she felt Rhett's hardening penis against her thigh. His arousal had happened so quickly that it'd shocked her. Desire brought a rush of moisture between her legs and she pressed her thighs together in an attempt to control the wet, pulsing flesh that made her feel as if she was coming out of her skin.

"Rh-ett!" His name had slipped from between trembling lips. She gasped again. One minute her feet were on the floor, then without warning Rhett had lifted her as effortlessly as if she were a small child, his arms tightening around her waist.

Denise looped her arms around his neck, holding him as if he were her lifeline. But Rhett Fennell wasn't her lifeline but the portal to where she could revisit her past—and hopefully get it right this time.

"Where are you going?" Rhett was striding across the living room.

"Where's your bedroom?"

"Why?"

Rhett stopped, meeting her eyes. "You're going to have to trust me, Denise. We lost six years because you didn't trust me, so tell me now what it is you want."

Denise buried her face between his neck and shoulder rather than gaze into the eyes that were able to see things she didn't want him to see. Rhett had known she'd fallen in love with him before she'd gotten up the nerve to tell him. His "I've known for a long time" had left her flustered *and* embarrassed, wondering if she'd been that transparent.

"I want us to start from the beginning, to pretend we just met and need to get to know each other better."

Rhett smiled. "That's not going to be easy, especially since I know what it's like to make love to you."

Her smile matched his. "Can't you pretend?"

"No, Denise. That's something I don't want to pretend about. Where's your bedroom?"

"It's down the hall and on your right."

Denise needed Rhett to make love to her, but she didn't want him to believe that she was desperate, that she'd been sitting around waiting for him to come back into her life. He'd had the distinct advantage when he'd blackmailed her into posing as his date and hostess and she'd been ready to trade her body to save her business, but not her heart. If they were to start over it would have to be the way it'd been when they'd met as college freshmen—as equals.

Rhett entered the bedroom and placed Denise on the queen-size bed, his body following hers down. Although the drapes were drawn, light was discernable through the diaphanous fabric. Moving with the agility of a large cat, he straddled her body, supporting his weight on his elbows.

He lowered his head, burying his face against the column of her scented neck. "Do you know how long I've wanted to do this?" he whispered in her ear.

Denise closed her eyes. Rhett had echoed her thoughts. She didn't want to feel him inside her as much as she'd wanted him to hold her. Sex she could have with any man, but it was the foreplay and afterplay that had made making love with Rhett so different from what she'd had with Kevin.

She uttered a small cry of protest when he rolled over. The breath caught in her throat when he stood up and unbuttoned his shirt and kicked off his shoes. Denise wanted to look away but couldn't when he unbuckled his belt and tossed it on a chair next to the bed. His slacks and briefs joined the belt, and with wide eyes, she stared at the muscles in his back and firm buttocks. She gasped again, this time when he turned to face her.

Denise had lost count of the number of times she'd viewed Rhett's nude body, but seeing it again made her aware of how beautifully proportioned it was. Years had added muscle and bulk to his lean frame. A smile parted her lips when he leaned over and kissed the end of her nose.

Rhett reached for the hem of her top, pulling it up and over her head. "Are you all right with this?" Denise closed her eyes, nodding. "Do you trust me not to do anything you don't want me to do?"

She opened her eyes. "Yes, Rhett, I trust you." It was the same thing he'd asked her before making love to her for the first time.

Slowly, methodically, he removed her clothes until she was as naked as he was. Gathering her off the mattress, he pulled back the duvet, placed her on the sheet and got into bed with her. He dropped an arm over her waist and pulled her closer until they were nestled like spoons.

"Are you okay, baby?"

Denise shifted into a more comfortable position. "I'm good, Rhett."

He swallowed a groan. "I'm not going to be so *good* in a minute."

"What's the matter?"

"I'm getting a hard-on, Denise, and unless you have some condoms on hand I suggest you stop wiggling."

"I don't."

"Neither do I," Rhett informed her.

"I thought most men carry condoms with them."

Rhett wanted to tell Denise he wasn't most men. Even when he'd become a serial dater he hadn't slept with *every* woman he'd asked out. The ones he'd slept with were still more than he'd anticipated before turning thirty.

"I guess I'm not like most men. If I'm not dating a woman, then I don't see a need to walk around with condoms in my pocket."

"Aren't you ever spontaneous?"

Rhett chuckled. "Is this your roundabout way of asking me if I ever had a one-night stand?"

Placing her hand over the large hand resting on her thigh, Denise smiled. "Yes."

"One-night stands can backfire. Remember what happened to Michael Douglas in *Fatal Attraction?*" He and Denise had what they'd called movie night. Either they would rent a movie or visit a movie house in Baltimore that featured retro films.

"How can I forget. But I don't blame the Glenn Close character as much as I do Michael Douglas's, because he was married and picking up a crazy woman was his punishment for cheating on his wife."

"She knew he was married when she invited him back to her place."

"So, that makes him exempt, Rhett?" Denise argued in a quiet voice.

"No, it doesn't. You know how I feel about men who cheat on their wives."

"But what about men who cheat on their girl-friends?"

"A girlfriend is not a wife, Denise."

"So, that makes it okay for him to cheat on her?"

"No, it doesn't make it okay. It's never okay once a man and woman are committed to each other."

"Then why—"

"Let's not rehash the past tonight," Rhett interrupted.

He pressed a kiss to the nape of her neck. "Please, baby."

Denise smiled, despite her annoyance. Rhett was right. If they were going to go forward, then they had to leave their past behind. "Okay, darling. You win—tonight."

"You just have to have the last word, don't you?"

"If you don't know me by now, then you'll never ever know me."

"Don't go Harold Melvin & the Blue Notes on me, Denise."

She giggled like a little girl. "So you recognize the lyrics. Remember when we used to play name the lyrics or the artist?"

"Yes, and you always won."

"That's because I didn't go to a stuffy old boarding school where all you heard was classical and chamber music. My parents played Motown and Philadelphia soul until I knew the words to every Stevie, Teddy and Temptations song."

Rhett's hand moved lower, his fingers grazing the down covering her mound. "That stuffy old boarding school was responsible for me getting into Johns Hopkins where I met this hot little sister who had my nose so wide open that a locomotive could fit with room to spare."

Denise had no comeback. She lay, listening to the sound of her own breathing until she closed her eyes and fell asleep.

## Chapter 8

"Come on, Denise. I'd like to get on the road before we get caught in traffic."

Hopping on her right foot, Denise pushed the left into the mate to the leather sandal. "I'm coming, Rhett. I had to comb my hair."

She'd applied what was left of a no-frizz serum to her wet hair and ran a wide-tooth comb through her damp hair in an attempt to tame the curls that were beginning to dry and swell like rising dough. Hopefully, she would be able to pick up another bottle of what she'd deemed her magic hair lotion at a drugstore chain once they got to Baltimore.

Rhett stood with his back to the door, arms crossed over his chest. He'd wanted to get up early and on the road before eight, but they'd overslept. They'd fallen asleep, then woke at midnight ravenous. The fridge was turned off, and the pantry bare, so they'd gotten dressed and went in search of an all-night diner where they'd ordered breakfast. It was after two when they returned to the apartment and went back to bed.

"Your hair looks fine."

She rolled her eyes at him, unable to believe he could look so virile in jeans, T-shirt, running shoes and a frayed baseball cap he should've discarded a long time ago. He'd showered but hadn't shaved.

"I don't like going out with wet hair."

Rhett angled his head and kissed her cheek. "It will dry before we get to Maryland."

"I know it will dry, but I'll end up looking like a Chia Pet."

"You'll just be a very beautiful Chia Pet," he teased.

"You'll say anything, Rhett, just to get your way."

His arms came down. "Is that really how you see me? That I'm all about coercion and manipulation?"

"We'll talk about it in the car," Denise countered, reaching for her keys. Rhett glared at her, then picked up their bags and opened the door. She locked the door, dropping the keys in the tote.

She knew Rhett was angry because she saw the nervous tic in his jaw when he'd clenched his teeth together. Denise didn't want to begin what was to become their second chance to get it right with a disagreement. The reason their college liaison had lasted for four years was because they were able to talk out their differences of opinion somewhat intelligently. Once they were committed, it hadn't become an off-and-on, now-and-then relationship. It was as if they were married, but only without the rings, license and officiant.

Although they had maintained separate dorms, once they'd begun sleeping together it was either at her dorm or Rhett's. The only time they did not sleep together was when she went home to Philadelphia and he returned to D.C.

They rode the elevator to the lobby and walked out into the brilliant late-spring sun. The streets of Penn's Landing were bustling with the activity of both vehicular and pedestrian traffic. It was as if after a long, unusually snowy winter, Philadelphians had emerged from their cabin-fever doldrums looking to take advantage of every sun-filled day Mother Nature granted them.

Rhett stored their bags in the trunk of the car, then touched the handle of the driver's-side door and opened it. He beckoned to Denise. "Come, beautiful. You're driving to Cape St. Claire."

Denise's mouth opened and closed several times as she digested his suggestion. He wanted *her* to drive *his* car to Maryland. She couldn't use the excuse that she didn't know how to get there because the vehicle was equipped with a high-tech navigational system. She slipped in behind the wheel, waiting until Rhett pushed a few buttons to adjust the seat to accommodate her shorter legs.

Hunkering down to her level, he ran the back of his hand over her cheek. "Do you need to adjust the back?"

She shook her head, flyaway curls moving as if they'd taken on a life of their own. "No, it's good."

"Make certain it's okay before I program it into the memory for you."

Resting her hands on the wheel, she extended her arms. "I think I'm going to need the back of the seat closer to my spine."

Rhett pushed a few more buttons and the pneumatic lumbar support cradled her back. He tapped another button and the three-position memory was set for Denise's proportions. Closing the door, he came around the car and sat beside her. He touched the Start Engine button, then quickly punched in the route to the house that had become his sanctuary.

It was on Cape St. Claire that he hadn't had to think about anything business-related. It was where he went to escape *and* to renew his spirit. Whenever he visited the covenanted unincorporated community he'd always been alone. Denise Eaton would become the first woman, other than Geraldine Fennell-Russell, who would cross the threshold of his waterfront refuge.

"Do you want me to put on some music?" he asked her as she backed out of the parking space.

"Yes."

Denise enjoyed the feel of the finely stitched leather on the hand-polished wood of the steering wheel under her fingers. The interior of the luxury car was designed for comfort, convenience and to soothe the senses with high-gloss burl walnut wood trim, glove-soft leather and an in-dash six-disc DVD/CD audio-video player.

The stiffness in her body eased as she followed the directions on the screen to the road leading to I-95. "I know what you're trying to do."

Stretching out long legs, Rhett pulled the beak of the hat lower over his forehead, then lowered the back of his seat into a reclining position. "What?"

"You know right well that after I drive your car I'm not going to want to drive Valentina ever again."

"You shouldn't be driving her at all, because you never know when she's going to break down at the most inopportune time."

"She is mechanically sound, Rhett. It's just that's she had a lot of mileage on her."

"I'd still feel better if you had a new car."

Her fingers tightened on the wheel. "I told you I'm going to buy a new one, but not until I sell my co-op."

Rhett gave her a sidelong glance from under the beak of his cap. "Do you want me to give you the down payment?"

"No!"

He raised his head, then fell back against the leather seat. "There's no need to get spastic, Denise."

"I'm not spastic, Rhett. It's just that I don't need your money."

"What if I lend you the down payment and you pay me back later?"

"No, no and no! Why are we arguing about money? We never did that before."

Touching a button, Rhett raised his seat back. "It's because I never had any. Your parents deposited money in your checking account every month, while I had to depend on what I'd earned from work study. It galled me whenever you suggested paying for dinner or a movie."

"We were college students, Rhett. We weren't expected to have a lot of money."

"You had money, Denise."

"Okay. I had more than you. Fast-forward six years and now you have more than I'd ever hope to earn in my lifetime." Denise shifted her eyes off the road for a couple of seconds. "I don't know why, but I feel your offer to buy me a car, or lend the money to buy one, is based on revenge and upmanship. I know you didn't like it when I suggested picking up the tab for dinner or a movie, but I thought you were all right with it when we agreed to take turns."

"I was never all right with it, Denise. Every time you

opened your wallet the words to TLC's 'No Scrubs' stayed with me for days."

Denise sucked her teeth. "You were hardly a scrub, Rhett Fennell. Every girl on campus knew who the scrubs were, but some were still willing to put up with them because they wanted a man. Even though my parents sent me an allowance, I still didn't have a lot of money. Xavier's undergraduate tuition was just under twenty thousand a year. He and I were in college at the same time, because he'd enrolled in The Citadel's graduate program. That put quite a strain on my parents' finances, but they made the sacrifice because they didn't want us to begin our careers burdened with student loans. That's why I refuse to accept any money from them to sustain the day care center."

"How did you buy your co-op without securing a mortgage?"

"When I was eight, I was involved in an auto accident when a car driven by a drunk driver jumped the curb, pinning me against a storefront. I wound up with a broken arm and a lot of bruises. Daddy sued the man, and the monies from the settlement were deposited in a custodial account. I was able to withdraw the monies that had earned quite a bit of interest after I'd graduated college. I'd taken your advice when you said the best investment anyone could make was in real estate, so I bought the co-op."

Rhett closed his eyes. Denise had trusted him enough to take his advice about investing in real estate, yet she hadn't when he'd sworn a solemn oath that he would never cheat on her. She'd claimed she believed him, but once the rumor started that he was sleeping with another coed, doubt had become her constant companion. He'd lost count of the number of times he'd tried to dissuade her from listening to gossip, but she wouldn't heed his warning. Then the rumor escalated and what was left of their fragile trust was shattered completely.

"What made you decide to start up your own business?"

Denise's sultry voice swept over him and he opened his eyes. He'd performed his work study at a Baltimore bank, where initially he was responsible for coding data for personal and business loans. The branch manager had promised to hire him after he'd graduated, but Rhett was faced with a dilemma when a headhunter from a major Philadelphia-based investment firm recruited him for their investment banking department, offering incentives such as full tuition reimbursement, bonuses and/or profit sharing. The only thing they wanted was a two-year commitment. He'd felt a particular loyalty to the bank, yet what the headhunter offered fit into his plan to pursue an MBA.

"It was a knee-jerk reaction," he said after a lengthy pause. "I was close to burnout from working and attending Wharton full-time. I'd mistakenly left the research paper I'd been developing for my thesis on my desk at work, and when I went into the office the next day it was missing."

Denise's hands tightened on the steering wheel when he mentioned Wharton. It wasn't until she'd read a profile on Garrett Fennell in *Black Enterprise* that she'd uncovered that Rhett had lived in Philadelphia while he'd attended Wharton School of the University of Pennsylvania. They'd lived in the same city yet they hadn't run into each other.

"Didn't you save it on a disk?"

"Yes, but it wasn't something I wanted made public until after I'd submitted it to my professor. Two weeks later all of the work I'd done was presented in what the banking division called developmental sessions. One of the vice presidents had claimed my work as his own."

"Did you confront him?"

Rhett snorted. "I did, but he claimed he'd been working on a similar strategy for more than a year. When I threatened to expose him, he said he had the power to fire me."

Denise gave Rhett another quick glance. "Please don't tell me he did."

Reaching over, he rested a hand on her right thigh. "Now, baby, you should know I don't scare that easily. I told him to fire me, but be prepared for a lawsuit, because my banking and finance professor had a draft of the paper. He asked me if I wanted to share credit on the strategy and I told him no. I think he was a little shocked at my response.

"The next day I came to him with a typed list of demands—I wanted out of my two-year contract without having to pay back the tuition, and I wanted my bonus in April rather than have to wait until December or early January. And I asked for a letter of recommendation for my next employer."

Denise laughed. "You were really ballsy, weren't you?"

"No more ballsy than the thieving bastard who stole my research paper."

She nodded. "You're right. Did you get what you wanted?"

"Yes. I graduated and moved back to D.C. I found a two-bedroom apartment where I set up a home office in the spare room. I'd always liked real estate better than investment banking, so I used a part of the bonus to buy a foreclosed property. The bank gave me a short-term, low-interest rehab loan and after it was brought up to code I sold it for three times what I'd paid for it.

"It took a while for me to build a relationship with the bank where I'd borrowed money, using what was in my account as collateral. The terms were if I repaid the loan in less than six months or a year, then the loan was interest-free."

"So, you've come to live up to the sobriquet as the Boy Wonder of Business."

Rhett frowned. He never liked the epithet, and disliked it more with each passing birthday. "It all comes down to common sense, Denise."

"I'm sure you've heard that common sense isn't all that common."

A smile replaced his frown. "You're right. Let me know when you get tired and I'll take over from you."

Denise narrowed her eyes at him. "I don't think so, Rhett. I *will* fight you if you try to get me from behind this wheel."

Rhett's fingers tightened slightly on her thigh under a pair of cropped cotton slacks. "There won't be much of a fight, baby girl. After all, I am a lot bigger than you."

"But I have a secret weapon, sweetheart."

"Which is?"

"I'm not telling. If I do, then it won't be a secret."

His hand moved up her thigh, the muscles tensing under his touch. "Will it hurt, baby?"

"The only thing I'm going to tell you is that you will enjoy it," Denise teased.

Throwing back his head, Rhett chanted, "Hurt me, hurt me please, baby."

Denise rested her hand right atop the one on her

**KIMANI ROMANCE**

# An Important Message from the Publisher

Dear Reader,

Because you've chosen to read one of our fine novels, I'd like to say "thank you"! And, as a special way to say thank you, I'm offering to send you two more Kimani™ Romance novels and two surprise gifts— absolutely FREE! These books will keep it real with true-to-life African American characters that turn up the heat and sizzle with passion.

Please enjoy the free books and gifts with our compliments...

*Glenda Howard*
For Kimani Press

*Peel off Seal and Place Inside...*

**EDITOR'S FREE GIFTS SEAL THANK YOU**

(JK-ROM-10R2)

We'd like to send you two free books to introduce you to Kimani™ Romance books. These novels feature strong, sexy women, and African-American heroes that are charming, loving and true. Our authors fill each page with exceptional dialogue, exciting plot twists, and enough sizzling romance to keep you riveted until the very end!

*KIMANI ROMANCE...LOVE'S ULTIMATE DESTINATION*

Your two books have a combined cover price of $13.98, but are yours **FREE!**

We'll even send you two wonderful surprise gifts. You can't lose!

## 2 FREE BONUS GIFTS!

*We'll send you two wonderful surprise gifts, (worth about $10) absolutely FREE just for giving KIMANI™ ROMANCE books a try! Don't miss out—MAIL THE REPLY CARD TODAY!*

Visit us online at www.ReaderService.com

# THE EDITOR'S "THANK YOU" FREE GIFTS INCLUDE:

Two Kimani™ Romance Novels
Two exciting surprise gifts

▶ If offer card is missing write to: The Reader Service, P.O. Box 1867, Buffalo, NY 14240-1867 or visit www.ReaderService.com ▶

thigh. "You just might get your wish. Tell me about where we're going and if it's casual or dressy."

"The cookout is hosted by a couple I met last year. She's an event coordinator and her husband is a pharmaceutical company executive. The gathering is casual, and if the weather holds, then we'll probably go out for a sail just before sunset."

"Do you have a boat?"

Rhett shook his head. "No, and I don't need one. I don't come to the Chesapeake enough to warrant owning a boat." He raised his seat back, changing the satellite radio station to one featuring soul music from the '70s and '80s.

Denise felt free, freer than she had for a very long time as cool air caressed her face from the car's vents. She sang along with Rhett, her alto blending and harmonizing with his baritone. She crossed the state line from Pennsylvania into Maryland, following the GPS from I-95 to I-895. Traffic wasn't as heavy and the landscape changed once she left the interstate for a rural road. It was half past twelve when she maneuvered down a narrowed paved road to Rhett's waterfront home. They had made one stop at Graul's Supermarket to buy perishables and other sundries for their brief stay on the Cape.

Rhett got out of the car and came around to assist Denise. He held her hand, while escorting her up the slate path leading to a two-story nineteenth-century Shingle Style house. Painted a cornflower-blue with white trim and shutters, it radiated warmth and charm. Lifting the handle on the doorknob, he punched in a code, disengaging the security system.

Rhett tugged at the curls falling over Denise's forehead. "Please wait here, while I check inside."

She sat on the stone step, staring out at century-old trees, ferns and wildflowers that seemingly grew naturally in wild abandon. However, when she looked closer she realized the plants were strategically arranged to give it the appearance of untamed wildness. There was also something about the house and surrounding landscape that made Denise feel as if she'd stepped back in time.

Glancing over her shoulder, she saw Rhett opening windows to take advantage of the breeze coming off the water. The house was built on a hill overlooking the Chesapeake.

"You can come in now," Rhett called out behind her.

Pushing to her feet, Denise kicked off her sandals, leaving them on the thick straw mat outside the front door, and walked into the house. A cherrywood console table flanked by bleached pine straight-back chairs and a large oval mirror filled the entryway hall. Her eyebrows lifted slightly when she saw the gaslight sconces on either side of the mirror, wondering if they worked or were there for decoration.

"They work, but instead of gas I had them wired for electricity."

Denise smiled at Rhett, who stood near the staircase leading to the second floor. "You read my mind."

He extended his hand. "Come, let me show you to your bedroom, then I'll bring everything in."

"Do you want me to help you?"

He shook his head. "No. I want you to relax before we leave. After all, you did drive down."

She barely caught a glimpse of the living room with oversize upholstered chairs in soft hues of cream and tan as she followed Rhett up the staircase. "How large is this house?"

"It was about sixty-six-hundred square feet, but the new addition added another twenty-two-hundred square feet. Originally there was only the entrance hall, living room, dining room, pantry, kitchen and two bedrooms and baths on the second floor. The architect replaced the two-story porch with a side entrance nestled below gables and dormers and expanded the area to include two more bedrooms with en suite baths. I'll give you a tour after I bring in the food." Rhett stopped at the end of the hallway with a colorful runner spanning its length. "This will be your bedroom."

Denise walked in, smiling. The room was large and sun-filled. There was something about the off-white furnishings that reminded her of the bedroom in her D.C. apartment. "It's very nice."

Rhett rested his hand at the small of her back. "You have your own en suite bathroom. My bedroom is on the other side of the pocket doors."

Tilting her head, Denise looked up at Rhett staring down at her. "What time do we have to leave?"

"Three. I wanted to get here early to give you time to unwind before we head out." He dropped a kiss on the riot of curls framing her face. "I'll be back."

Waiting until he walked out of the room, Denise walked over to the windows. The view was so breathtakingly beautiful that she felt a lump form in her throat. She tried imagining looking out on the churning waters during a storm or the sky obliterated by falling snow. Swallowing, she tried to relieve the constriction in her dry throat.

Rhett had accomplished everything he'd set out to do, while she was still a work-in-progress. There was the matter of securing the grant for her after-school program; and once that was up and running her next project was to set up a private school for at-risk boys.

What Denise found ironic was there was no allowance for romance in her plan for the future, and that meant she had to enjoy whatever time she had with Rhett. They were given the opportunity for a do-over and she planned to make the best of it while it lasted.

## Chapter 9

Denise felt like a kid at summer camp when she discovered the en suite bathroom was designed like a mini-spa. A garden tub with a Jacuzzi, free-standing shower and a sunken hot tub, surrounded by a water-impervious wood floor, was the perfect setting for total relaxation. She smiled. Now she knew why Rhett wanted her to relax.

Walking across the space, she opened the French doors to reveal another set of doors that opened onto a balcony overlooking a sizeable semicircular terrace off the main floor. Moving closer to the edge of the balcony, she rested her arms along the railing and closed her eyes. The warmth of the sun, the cool breeze off the bay and the smell of the water swept over her like a magical concoction, renewing and reviving her.

It had been so long, much too long, since Denise had been able to kick back and relax. Attending family gatherings didn't count, because they only lasted a day or two at the most. She hadn't taken a real vacation since opening the center, and long weekends didn't count. Her entire existence was wrapped up in making a go of New Visions, and she hadn't realized how staid her life had become until now.

Rhett had become a master at buying, renovating and flipping properties, and yet he still took time out to relax. Denise opened her eyes. There had to be something wrong with her. She was working very hard but not very smart. It wasn't as if she didn't have anything to show for her sacrifice—the progressive child care center was a model that she was very proud of. Maybe, she mused, reuniting with Rhett was what she needed to gain some insight into what she'd been doing and needed to do.

Rhett had talked about burnout when he'd attended Wharton full-time while working full-time. Maybe it was fatigue that had made him less than alert when he'd left his research paper on his desk at work. Fatigue that had been the impetus to change him *and* his future after his boss had claimed the work Rhett had done as his. It had been enough to fuel his rage where he'd been able to shake off the complacency and strike out on his own—something he'd talked about incessantly when they'd been in college together.

Even when she'd told Rhett that she wanted to follow in the footsteps of her mother, aunts and cousins to become a teacher, he'd asked her whether she wanted to spend the next thirty years of her life in a classroom. When she hadn't answered he'd continued, asking whether she would consider becoming a principal or even a superintendent.

Rhett had always told her to aim high, and every five years reassess where she was and where she'd want to go. It had taken less than four years of classroom teaching before Denise knew she wanted to open a child care center. Teachers were hired to educate, and she wanted to blend education with what she'd recognized as missing in so many young children coming into school for the first time—social skills.

Many were lacking manners, the tools to work and play well with their peers and too many were willing to settle disputes with their hands rather than with their brain. The children at New Visions were tutored in setting the table, how to eat and clean up after themselves. There were rewards for good behavior and isolation from the others in their group for negative behavior. A three-year-old sitting alone at a table for three minutes while his or hers friends were engaged in play was akin to a life of solitary confinement.

The benchmark for New Visions was love. Love of themselves, their parents, family, neighborhood and country. Her teachers stressed the concept that if you loved someone or something you protected it. Praise was heaped upon the children like rain soaking the earth in order for flowers to grow. Praise and positive reinforcement were in short supply from parents who were dealing with their own stress of keeping their jobs, while attempting to keep their families intact.

The children at New Visions were her children and her babies, and everyone connected to the center had become extended family. Denise opened her eyes to see Rhett, as he carried and set down the frame of a round rattan table on the terrace below. She stood there long enough to see him bring out a quartet of matching chairs before she closed the doors and retreated to the bedroom. She found her bag and tote next to the door.

*My bedroom is on the other side of the pocket doors.*

His words echoed in her head. He'd given her a choice. Either she could sleep in her own bedroom or share his bed.

What Denise hadn't wanted was a choice. She wouldn't have thought him brash or arrogant if he'd taken her overnight bag to his bedroom only because she wanted *and* needed Garrett Mason Fennell to remind her why she'd been born female. She didn't so much want to make love with Rhett—she needed to make love with him, desperately.

Closing the door, she picked up her bags and carried them over to the dressing area. Emptying the contents, she hung them up in a walk-in closet with racks, shelves and drawers constructed with a shopaholic in mind. Even her extensive shoe collection would look lost in the expansive closet.

Denise hung up a pair of navy-blue raw silk slacks she'd planned to wear with a white silk kimono piped in navy with a blue and white-striped obi sash that was an exact match for her three-inch, peep-toe espadrilles. Despite putting in ten- and sometimes twelve-hour workdays, she always took time to pamper herself with a weekly mani/pedi and monthly hydrating facial and full-body massage. Each and every time she left the salon she thought of her mother. Paulette Eaton had taken her daughter to her favorite salon at six for a mini-day of beauty. Denise had been awed by sights and smells associated with a salon and the first time she stuck her chubby brown toes and fingers in bowls of soapy warm water she was hooked!

She and her mother continued their weekly mother/daughter spa dates until she left Philly for Baltimore. After conferring with her father, Denise had given her mother an all-expenses-paid vacation to a golfing/spa retreat in Sedona, Arizona, for her fiftieth birthday.

Leaning over, Denise examined her toes for chips in the candy-apple-red polish. Removing the rubber shower shoes from her tote, she slipped her feet into them. Nothing ruined a pedicure like walking barefoot.

She checked her watch. She had less than two hours to wind down from the drive and prepare for the afternoon and evening festivities. Gathering a set of underwear, Denise returned to the bathroom to take a leisurely bath.

Rhett finished setting up the deck furniture that had been stored in the three-car garage. When he'd purchased the house it had been abandoned for years following the death of an elderly couple whose children had relocated to the west coast. Jeff McNeill, one of the partners at the architectural firm that drew up all the plans for his renovated properties, had called to let him know about the house scheduled to be sold at auction for delinquent taxes.

Rhett had cancelled all of his meetings and driven up to see the house. It had weathered drastically over the years and was perilously close to the point where it would have to be demolished. Jeff's recommendation had been to strip it to the bare bones. His plans had included replacing the two-story porch with a new addition that increased the square footage by two thousand. Jeff had also added a pair of French doors opening to a series of terraces to take advantage of the water views. Older spaces had been reworked and expanded, including raising the ceiling in the master bedroom, adding en suite bathrooms and an extra bedroom.

Utilizing the services of his favorite interior design

firm, Rhett had given them carte blanche when it came to furnishing the interiors. They had been aware of his personal tastes, and the result had been a home designed for living and entertaining.

The first morning he'd woken and walked ten feet to look out over Chesapeake Bay, Rhett had known it was a scene he wanted to repeat over and over. In that instant he'd known this was a house he wouldn't flip, but live in for the rest of his life. It wasn't a house, but his home.

Moving around the ultra-modern kitchen, he brewed a pot of iced tea and removed the cellophane from a freshly made Caesar salad he'd picked up from the supermarket's deli section. Smaller containers held large cooked shrimp, cubes of smoked chicken and thinly sliced roast beef.

His cooking skills were still less than stellar, but Rhett had mastered the art of cooking breakfast. All he needed was a stovetop grill, because he was able to keep an eye on grilling bacon or sausage, home fries and eggs at the same time. It was when he had to shift from the grill to the stove and/or the oven that he tended to burn or overcook something. And there was never the likelihood that he would go hungry as long as there were stores that offered prepared meals. He tended to avoid fast-food restaurants in favor of those serving cook-to-order dishes.

Rhett stepped back surveying the table that flowed into a cooking island in the all-white and stainless-steel kitchen. Turning on his heels, he went in search of Denise, bumping into her as she walked in. He caught her before she lost her balance.

"Oops!"

"Sorry, baby. I was just coming to get you." He

and Denise had spoken in unison. "I just put together something to tide us over until later this evening." It'd been twelve hours since they'd eaten breakfast at the diner.

Denise walked into the kitchen, her mouth gaping in stunned amazement. Stark-white vinyl tiles bordered in gray set the stage for a large space with rows of recessed lights in a ceiling of crown molding. Walk-in freezer, French-door refrigerator, sub-zero freezer, wine cabinet and built-in television, double ovens with warming drawers and cooktop stove and grill made the space a chef's dream. A triple sink at the opposite end of a countertop with three high stools with steel frames was the perfect place to sit or eat, while surveying the activity going on in the magnificent kitchen. Fine custom cabinetry without handles or hardware provided a sleekness and uninterrupted wall of pristine white. The tall, narrow vents over the stove did double duty. They were constructed to look like cabinets but were designed to pull all cooking odors out of the kitchen. The light from a ceiling fixture with ten conical spheres, suspended from steel rods over the dining countertop, reflected off the shiny surface like polished silver.

Her smile was dazzling once she recovered. "Now, this is a kitchen."

Wrapping an arm around her waist, Rhett pulled Denise gently over to the table. "You like it?"

"I love it, Rhett." *What's not to love,* she thought. It was the perfect place in which to plan a dinner party. "The house is immaculate," she said, glancing at Rhett over her shoulder when he seated her. "Who cleans it?"

Rhett sat beside Denise, reaching for the pitcher of tea and filling a tall glass with the cold liquid. He placed a dish with sliced lemons and another covered dish filled with sugar next to her plate.

"Whenever I know I'm coming up, I call a local cleaning service to let them know what time I expect to arrive. Once I'm here I'll call and they send someone over. There's not a lot to do—dusting, vacuuming, cleaning the bathrooms and occasionally changing the beds."

Denise took a sip of her tea before adding a teaspoon of sugar. "How often do you come here?"

"Not often enough. But that's going to change this summer. My mother and her husband come up at least once a month, so the house doesn't remain vacant for too long a period. Speaking of my mother, I told her that I'd run into you again, and she sends her best."

Picking up a cloth napkin and spreading it over her lap, Denise kept her gaze fixed on her plate. "Tell her same here."

"You can tell her next week."

Shifting, Denise turned to give Rhett an incredulous look. "What's next week?"

"She's coming to stay for a week. Unfortunately you won't get to meet her husband because he has to attend a conference in Dallas."

"What is she going to say about me staying with you?"

"What do you want her to say, Denise? That she doesn't approve of her son bringing a woman into *his* home? Look, baby, my mother stopped monitoring what I did and who I was with a long time ago. I didn't know she was seeing anyone seriously until she called to tell me she was getting married. I don't get into Geraldine Russell nee Fennell's business and she doesn't get into mine."

"Unlike mine," Denise mumbled.

Rhett picked up the salad greens with shaved parmesan cheese and placed it in a bowl at her place setting. "I understand your mother and what she wants."

"And that is?" she asked, spearing several shrimp and placing them in her salad, before spooning the dressing over the romaine lettuce.

"She wants grandchildren."

"So do a lot of parents, but they usually aren't so blatant and vocal about it."

"Lighten up on Paulette, darling. Gerri's no different. It's just that she's more subtle with her hints. She's like, 'Garrett, baby. You know it's not good for a man to spend so much time alone.' Or it's 'Look, son, I'm not getting any younger and I'd like to have a few grandchildren before I die.' That's when I tell her to stop the melodrama. Gerri's not even fifty and she's in good health, so I don't believe she's going to expire anytime soon."

"What's up with parents wanting grandchildren? You think they would've had enough of kids when they had to raise their own children."

"I suppose we'll find out what it's all about once we raise our children."

Rhett realized too late what he'd said when Denise stared at him as if he were a complete stranger. He opened his mouth to correct himself and then decided against it. What he'd said had come from his heart. He wanted children, and he wanted Denise Eaton to be the mother of their children.

"I didn't ask you to come here because I was hoping you would sleep with me," he said instead.

"Why did you ask me?"

Rhett knew what he was about to admit to Denise

would either shatter their fragile truce or bring them closer together, because the harder he'd tried to ignore the truth the more it continued to haunt him. Every woman he'd met and/or slept with had become her. He'd searched in vain to find a modicum of what he'd shared with Denise in them—but had failed miserably. It was why he'd begun what had become a revolving door of women coming and going out of his life.

He placed his left hand over her right, holding it firmly lest she flee the kitchen. "I love you, Denise. I don't care about you and Trey—"

"Don't mention his name," Denise practically shouted, cutting Rhett off. "Please," she whispered hoarsely. "This time it's only *us,* Rhett."

He lowered his head and his voice. "You know what this means, Denise?" She nodded, her head going up and down like a bobblehead doll. "This time it's for keeps. And, when I put a ring on your finger it's never coming off. Do you understand?" She nodded again. "Is there anything you'd like to add?"

A strength came to Denise she hadn't thought possible. They'd reached the point where their relationship would be resolved by a lifetime of commitment and fidelity. "Yes. There is something I'd like you to do."

"Just say it, baby, and if it's within my power I'll make it happen."

Denise closed her eyes against his intense stare. "Make love to me."

The request was barely off her tongue when she was swept off the stool and carried across the kitchen. She hadn't realized she was holding her breath until she felt the constriction across her chest. She was shaking, from head to toe, and there was nothing Denise could do to stop the tremors.

She'd wanted and needed Rhett every night of their six-year separation. There were times when she'd caught herself searching restaurants, clubs and stores for his face. Every time she'd seen a tall, black man who looked even remotely like the one to whom she'd given her heart, she'd had to stop and make certain it wasn't him before going about her business.

Men who'd expressed an interest in her and had worked enough nerve to ask her out asked whether she was into men when she turned them down. That had been the reason she'd decided to go out with Kevin. It had been the only time she'd dated out of her race, so she'd seen him as safe. The single physical encounter between them had become a disaster—for both. Unable to fake her response, Denise had just lain there waiting for him to finish. Kevin, sensing her nonparticipation, had aborted the act, put his clothes on and went home. The next time they'd met it had been to say goodbye.

Denise tightened her grip around Rhett's neck as he carried her up the staircase and down the hallway to the adjoining bedrooms. He strode past the door to the one he'd assigned her and into his. She wasn't given the opportunity to view the furnishings when she found herself sprawled over a large bed with a decoratively carved mahogany headboard.

Her gaze met and fused with Rhett's as he pulled the T-shirt over his head, then unsnapped his jeans, pushing them and his briefs off his hips in one smooth motion. Her pulse quickened, her breathing becoming shallow as her gaze lowered to his muscular thighs, and she found she couldn't look away from his enormous erection. But she did close her eyes when a rush of wetness left her panting as if she'd run a grueling race.

This was what she'd been waiting for, waiting for

Garrett Fennell to come back into her life and remind
her why she'd been born female. All her senses took over
when his knee touched the side of the bed, causing the
mattress to dip slightly. Her chest rose and fell heavily
when he divested her of her clothes. His hands were
steady, fingers nimble. She smiled. He'd always made
undressing her as much a part of foreplay as kissing,
touching and caressing. Holding up her arms, Denise
wasn't disappointed when Rhett moved over her, his
welcoming weight pressing her down to the mattress.

Rhett's nose nuzzled her ear as he trailed light kisses
along the column of her scented neck. He'd fantasized
about making love to Denise so often that he wasn't
certain where reality began and fantasy ended. But it
was about to end—now. She was real and everything
that made Denise Eaton who she was flooded his
consciousness—her scent, the texture of her skin, soft
sounds escaping her parted lips. He lay between her
silken thighs, his blood-engorged penis pulsing against
her belly.

"Rhett?"

"What is it, baby?"

"Do you have protection?"

His heart felt like a stone in his chest when he heard
Denise's query. Although he had condoms he didn't want
to use them, because he wanted to marry her and get
her pregnant as quickly as humanly possible.

"Yes. Why?"

"I don't want to get pregnant."

Rhett wanted to ask her if she ever wanted to get
pregnant, but decided it would open a dialogue that was
certain to kill the moment. "Let me know when you
want to start a family and I'll do everything I can to
oblige."

She laughed softly. "Why do you make it sound as if you'd be doing me a favor?"

"It's not about that, Denise."

"What is it about?"

There was a long pause. "It's about us being on the same page. I have to want what you want when you want it. I can't want a child when you don't."

Curving her arms under Rhett's shoulders, Denise pressed a kiss to his warm throat when he raised his head. "I want a baby, darling. It just can't be now. And aren't you forgetting something?"

"What's that?"

"I have no intention of becoming a baby mama." Denise watched Rhett's expression change from desire to one that had become a mask of stone.

"You claim I've changed. But there's one thing about me that will never change and that is I will never get a woman pregnant and not marry her. Speaking of marriage," he continued without pausing to take a breath, "when do you want to get married?"

Things were happening so quickly that she felt as if she were on a merry-go-round of emotions. It hadn't been a week since she and Rhett had reunited and he'd picked up as if time had stood still for them. It was the same question he'd asked her six weeks before their graduation and her response had been she didn't know. Dating Garrett Fennell had been one thing and becoming Mrs. Denise Fennell within weeks of her college graduation had been something she hadn't been able to fathom at that time. What Rhett hadn't known was that her ambivalence had stemmed from the rumors that he was sleeping with her and another woman at the same time.

"New Year's Eve." It was the first date that popped into her head.

Rhett blinked. "You want to wait that long?"

"It's only seven months away. It's going to take that long to plan a wedding if we're going to do it right."

A smile broke through his expression of uncertainty. "Okay. New Year's it is."

Denise closed her eyes. "Now that we've done enough talking do you still intend to make love to me?"

"Do I have a hard-on, Ms. Eaton?"

"How do you do that?"

"Do what?"

"Sustain an erection without going inside me. Are you taking a pill for erectile dysfunction?"

Without warning, Rhett flipped Denise over on her belly, pulling her up to her knees. "I told you one day your mouth is going to get you in trouble, and today is that day."

Denise struggled to free herself, but she was no match for Rhett's superior strength. He managed to hold her while reaching over to the drawer in the bedside table and removing a condom. Using his teeth, he tore open the packet, removed the latex sheath and rolled it down the length of his penis.

He knew she didn't like this position, because he was able to control their lovemaking. Rhett also knew it gave her maximum pleasure when with every stroke his penis rubbed against her clitoris, making her come too quickly. Repressing an orgasm as long as possible assured her maximum sexual satisfaction.

"No, darling," Denise pleaded.

Rhett kissed the nape of her neck. "I'm not going to hurt you, baby."

She knew he wasn't going to hurt her, but she didn't

want it to be over before it began. But it did begin when she felt his hardness searching between the folds to find her wet and ready for his possession. Gasps overlapped moans as her celibate flesh stretched slowly to take every long, delicious inch of him until he was fully sheathed inside her.

Rhett couldn't remember Denise that tight, that small. All he knew was he'd come home. Her flesh held him tightly then eased only to repeat it again and again until the fire between her thighs spread to his, dissolving both in an inferno from which there was no escape. He covered her breasts, squeezing the firm globes gently, his hips pushing against hers as she pushed back against his groin.

Her breathing changed, becoming deeper. Her gasps turned into deep surrendering moans of unrestrained pleasure. Sounds of erotic pleasure became unrestrained screams of ecstasy when Denise stiffened with the explosive rush of orgasmic fulfillment sweeping over her. She lost count of the number of orgasms after three, succumbing to the uncontrolled passion that shattered into a million little pieces.

Rhett's release had come too quickly; he'd thought he could hold back but he couldn't. It'd been too long since he and Denise had been together. It was as if he'd been starving for weeks and someone had escorted him to the banquet table, urging him to eat whatever he wanted. Instead of nibbling he'd gorged until he couldn't move, too emotionally drained to speak.

Still joined, he turned her over, tucking her under him. Cradling her face, he placed a kiss on the bridge of her nose. "This one was for me. The next one will be for you."

Eyes closed, Denise's lips parted in a smile. She ran

her fingertips up and down Rhett's moist back. "Wrong, Rhett. This one was for me, too."

They lay together, talking quietly as they'd done when they'd shared a much smaller bed in sparsely furnished bedrooms. It was with great reluctance that Rhett pulled out, moved off the bed and went into the bathroom to discard the condom. When he returned Denise had turned on her side, the sheet pulled up over her breasts. He joined her in bed, pressing his chest to her back.

"I love you," he whispered softly.

Hot tears pricked the backs of Denise's eyes. Rhett loved her and she loved him. It wasn't his love she doubted, but her ability to trust him to be faithful to her. However, time was on her side. She had a little more than seven months to put him to the test.

## Chapter 10

Denise moved closer to Rhett when they were greeted by their hostess. Brooke Andersen was tall, thin, blonde, tanned and looked as if she'd stepped off the glossy pages of a Ralph Lauren ad.

Brooke extended her hands, the ray of the sun reflecting off the many bracelets with precious and semiprecious stones on her slender wrists. The size of the diamond in her engagement ring and the channel-set diamonds in the eternity band were a blatant show of grandiosity. It was hard to pinpoint her age. Advances in cosmetic surgery seemingly had frozen time for the nipped and tucked woman.

"Rhett, darling. I'm so glad you could come," Brooke purred like a satisfied feline. "We'll be boarding in about ten minutes." Her bright blue eyes shifted to Denise. "Aren't you lovely? And what a darling outfit."

Denise gave the woman a too-sweet smile. "Thank you so much."

Rhett wrapped an arm around Denise's waist. "Denise, Brooke Andersen. Brooke, Denise Eaton."

Brooke beckoned her husband. "Jim, darling. Rhett has arrived."

Rhett exchanged an amused look with Denise, wondering if she'd found Brooke as entertaining as he did. He'd always found her to be a little over-the-top, but whenever he needed her to coordinate an event for him she would clear her calendar and make it happen.

He and Denise had lingered in bed, dozing off and on. They'd shared a shower before going down to the kitchen to salvage the remains of their aborted meal. He knew it was too late to show up to eat at the Andersens, because the invitation had stated it would be a sit-down dinner; however, Rhett had called Jim to inform him that he wouldn't arrive in time to eat, but would be there before the *Elena Victoria* sailed.

Jim Andersen, dressed in white linen like his wife and most of their guests, made his way toward them. Physically, he was Brooke's counterpart. The only difference was his hair was silver to her platinum-blond. He flashed a toothy grin. "Garrett, I'm so glad you made it."

After Rhett introduced her to their host, Denise took note of the people, the Andersens' home and the yacht moored off the pier. The sprawling Georgian Colonial was magnificent, as were the grounds on which it sat. Every blade of grass in the manicured lawn was exactly the same length. When Rhett had mentioned they were going to attend a cookout she thought there would be lots of people and that it wouldn't be a sit-down affair with a waitstaff picking up and setting down different courses.

When her family members hosted a cookout the only sitting was when everyone filled their plates and they needed someplace to set it in order to eat without spilling the contents. What Brooke Andersen needed was a generous dose of reality. Rhett mentioned he'd invited the Andersens and a few of his neighbors to his house the following weekend. Geraldine would also be in attendance, so between the two of them they would give the supercilious Cape St. Claire residents another version of a cookout.

Crew members were carrying crates to the boat as several other couples were arriving. They were younger and more outgoing. The men tapped their BlackBerries, while their female counterparts were texting or listening to their iPods. Two twenty-something women called Brooke mother and Jim father. More cars were maneuvering onto the property as friends of the Andersen children greeted one another with shrieks and laughter.

Rhett noticed the direction of Denise's gaze. Leaning closer, he dipped his head, pressing his mouth to her ear. "Now the fun begins."

"I hear you," she whispered when two men sporting colorful shirts with Hawaiian prints carried audio equipment down the pier to the gleaming white boat bobbing on the water. The younger Andersens had brought along a DJ.

The fun began as soon as the anchor to the sleek 128-foot yacht lifted, and it moved smoothly on the surface of the water. A bar was set up in the bridge deck's sky lounge that was used as a game room and theater. Between the pulsing beat of music ranging from hip-hop, rock and pop, drinks flowed, and a lively card game was in progress, while crew members circulated carrying trays of hot and cold finger foods.

Brooke, who'd appointed herself Denise's chaperone, took her on a tour of the sailing vessel designed with an emphasis on relaxed comfort. She called the *Elena Victoria* her country house party at sea. The ship was staffed by a crew of nine, with three decks of cabins and salons. There were four guest staterooms, a master suite and tender tucked into the aft that opened to become a swimming platform and dock. She proudly announced that the length of the ship qualified it as a superyacht. The interiors were luxurious. Walnut, teak, a gleaming stainless-steel stair on the aft main deck, ebony-and-nickel-accented oak tables bespoke elegance and a grace of style seen in the finest homes.

Brooke stared at the woman who'd accompanied Garrett Fennell. She was more than lovely. She'd fashioned her hair into a chignon; the style was perfect for her Asian-inspired outfit. One of her friends, although much older than Garrett, had asked her to invite him with the hope that he would be receptive to her subtle advances. But the woman was so disappointed when Brooke informed her that the young entrepreneur was bringing someone with him that she took to her bed, feigning a migraine.

"Jim and I are sailing to the Mediterranean this year without the children," Brooke intoned. "I told him I wanted to see the Baltic and cruise the fjords, and see St. Petersburg but only if there's time."

"The *Elena Victoria* is a spectacular ship," Denise complimented without guile. From the leather-topped desk in the study adjacent to the master stateroom to the carefully decorated guest cabins and pieces of art, the yacht was the epitome of safety, comfort and beauty.

Brooke managed what passed for a smile when the muscles in her face refused to move. "I know Garrett is always tied up with one deal or another, but try to convince your boyfriend to come along when we sail down to the Caribbean for a week before the tropical storm season begins."

"I'll talk to him," Denise promised.

"Speaking of your handsome boyfriend, I see him looking for you. Please apologize to him if I've monopolized too much of your time."

Denise mumbled she would as she made her way over to where Rhett was standing near the rail, seemingly half listening to something Brooke's daughter was telling him. His expression changed when their eyes met. She recognized what he was trying to communicate to her.

Walking over to him, she slipped her arm through his. "I'm sorry to interrupt, but I need to borrow my fiancé for a few minutes." The word *fiancé* seemed to get the woman's attention, and she turned and walked away.

"Let's go up on the upper deck," Rhett said sotto voce, as he led her away from the crowd and up a flight of stairs. The view from the top of the yacht was spectacular. There was a near full moon and without the lights from high-rise buildings the stars appeared brighter, closer.

Wrapping his arms around Denise's waist, he pulled her to his chest while sharing his body's heat. "Are you cold, darling?"

Burying her face against his chest, she shook her head. "No. I'm good." Her top had long sleeves.

"I should've warned you that Brooke's rather chatty *and* clingy."

Denise smiled. "She's okay as long as I don't have to deal with her every day. Speaking of every day, she wants me to convince you to go along with her and Jim when they sail down to the Caribbean in a couple of weeks."

"I'd go if you could get away."

"I can't, Rhett. Our enrollment numbers increase during the summer recess. And then there are employee vacations, so we'll be stretched pretty thin over the next couple of months."

"When do you take your vacation?"

"I don't."

Pulling back, Rhett stared at Denise with an incredulous look on his face. "You're kidding, aren't you?"

She closed her eyes and shook her head. "No. I haven't had a vacation in more than two years."

Grasping her shoulders, he shook her gently. "Have you lost your mind? How long do you think you can keep going without taking a break?"

"I get a break."

"When?"

"Remember, I don't work weekends," she argued softly.

"Weekends aren't enough, Denise."

"They're enough for me, Rhett. I sleep until late morning and then laze around for most of the day."

"When do you shop for food?"

"I do that during the week before I go home."

"How about laundry?"

"I have a washer and dryer in my apartment."

"Do you cook for yourself?"

"Of course I do."

"When?" Rhett asked, continuing with his interrogation.

"Usually on Sundays I cook enough to last me until midweek. After that, I'll either bring something in or order takeout."

"Who cleans your apartment?"

"I do."

"Do you hear yourself, Denise? You cook, clean, shop and do laundry. And that's when you're not at the center. When are you going to make time for Denise?"

She frowned. "I don't know what you're talking about."

"When do you find the time to do what you like to do? I remember the girl who loved going to the movies and art galleries. You used to drag me to every museum whenever they had a new exhibit. When was the last time you went to a museum?"

"I don't remember."

"Of course you don't," Rhett countered, "because it probably was with me. I'm going to give you an early birthday gift of a cleaning service and personal chef."

"No, Rhett!"

"Yes, Denise! I don't want to marry a shell of a woman come the end of the year."

Her temper flared. "Now I know what this is all about. You want me nice and perky when you flaunt me as Mrs. Garrett—"

"That's enough, Denise."

"It's not enough, Garrett. You can't come back into my life and turn it upside down without first talking to me. I'm not a piece of property you've bought, then you have to decide whether you'll either keep it or unload it for a profit. When I marry you I want to be your partner.

I'm not some hapless creature who can't think or take care of herself."

"I didn't mean for it to come out like that."

"Well, it did. If I'm awarded the grant, then there will be enough money to hire an assistant director, and that will free me up to take a vacation."

"Why didn't you say that?"

"You didn't ask, Rhett. You just started firing questions at me and—"

"I'm sorry. Will you forgive me?"

"I'll think about it, but only if you dance with me."

Rhett listened to the music drifting up from below deck. The DJ was playing one of their favorite songs. Taking her in his arms, he tucked her curves into his body. They danced without moving their feet, their bodies swaying sensuously from side to side.

"I want to make love to you right here," he rasped in her ear.

"We can't," Denise whispered.

"Why not, baby?"

"What if someone sees us?"

Rhett laughed. "Everyone onboard is an adult. I'm certain they're all quite familiar with copulating."

"That may be so, but I'm not going to copulate in a public place."

"Where's your sense of adventure, baby?" His hands cradled her hips, allowing her to feel his hard-on. "I'm in pain, sweetheart."

"It would serve you right if I jerked you off right here," Denise teased.

Throwing back his head, Rhett laughed loudly. "Damn, girl. When did you get so nasty?"

"You were the one who turned me into a bad girl."

He sobered quickly. "You're right about that. But I

have to say that you were an excellent student. You were also a quick study."

Denise buried her face between his neck and shoulder. "That's because you were an incredible teacher."

"Do you think you'll need additional tutoring?"

"A little. But you better get all of the tutoring in tonight because I'm expecting my period."

"When?"

"Tomorrow."

"I'll see if I can fit you into my busy schedule."

Denise shivered as if someone had run a feather over the back of her neck. Rhett was talking about fitting her in. Was he referring to his sleeping with another or other women?

"Who else are you sleeping with?"

Rhett stopped swaying. "What!?"

"Don't what me, Garrett."

"Don't tell me we're going to rehash old crap, Denise."

"It's not old crap. I need to know if you're sleeping with me and another woman at the same time."

"No!"

"Don't raise your voice to me."

Rhett dropped his arms. "When I speak in a normal tone you seem not to hear me."

"I hear you."

"No, you don't, or you never would've asked me something so damned asinine. I told you the first time I made love with you that I've never been able to sleep with more than one woman at the same time. Emotionally I'm not equipped to play bed-hopping games. You not trusting me is what drove us apart. Why are you doing it again?"

Denise realized she didn't have a comeback. She

moved over to the rail, peering out into the water. Why, she mused, couldn't she let go of the past? Closing her eyes, she leaned back against Rhett when he came up behind her.

"I'm sorry, Rhett."

Wrapping his arms around her midriff, he kissed the side of her neck. "Apology accepted. And I'm sorry I raised my voice to you."

She smiled. "Apology accepted."

They lost track of time as they stood together, each lost in their private thoughts. When they went below deck they found everyone in the sky lounge watching a movie. All of the chairs were occupied and those who hadn't found a chair sat on the carpet. Rhett found a spot, pulling Denise down to sit between his outstretched legs. It was a romantic comedy he'd seen before, but he enjoyed viewing it again.

The ship sailed down the intercoastal waterway to Chesapeake Ranch Estates before reversing its course. It was after three when Rhett pressed the remote that opened the garage door. He drove in and shut off the engine, closing the door behind him.

"I can't believe it's so late," Denise said around the yawn she covered with her hand when Rhett helped her out of the car.

"Did you enjoy yourself?"

"Yes, I did."

"I'm glad."

He was glad and she was glad she'd agreed to spend the weekend with Rhett. "I'm going upstairs to shower and get into bed before I fall asleep standing up."

Rhett winked at her. "I'll be up in a few minutes."

The few minutes became forty minutes, and when he walked into his bedroom Denise was sound asleep. He took a shower to get rid of the saltwater smell clinging to his clothes and body. Denise stirred but didn't wake up when he got into bed with her.

She didn't know how serious he'd been when he told her about the cleaning service and personal chef. Perhaps he'd presented it all wrong, but Rhett knew he had to try to convince Denise to slow down before she broke down mentally and physically.

He'd been there, done that when working and attending classes full-time. There were mornings when he'd had to force himself to get out of bed. The theft of his research paper had been a blessing in disguise. If the greedy bastard hadn't taken it there was no doubt he would still be working for the investment banking firm.

Rhett knew he had to find a way to help New Visions financially, so as to give Denise respite from the sole responsibility of the child care center. He knew she wouldn't accept a check from him outright, but she'd be a fool to reject money from a local company willing to make a charitable donation.

His mind was spinning with ideas when fatigue won out, and he joined Denise in sleep.

As predicted, Denise saw evidence of her menses, accompanied by cramps and a headache. She spent the afternoon reclining on the chaise on the terrace, sipping lukewarm tea with lemon. She tolerated the cramps because her period only lasted three days. Any more than that and she would be forced to take something to alleviate the pain. During the drive back to D.C., she was practically monosyllabic, preferring to sleep than talk.

Rhett, who was more than familiar with the change

in Denise's mood, didn't pressure her to talk. He found a space in the visitor section of the parking lot adjacent to her building and he carried her bags when they rode the elevator to her apartment.

"Do you want me to hang out with you tonight?" he asked when she unlocked the door.

Denise turned and stared up at Rhett. He hadn't bothered to shave and the stubble on his lean face enhanced his blatant masculinity. "Do you want to?"

He angled his head, smiling. "Yes."

"Come in."

Rhett kissed her forehead. "Let me go back to the car and get my bag." He winked at her. "Don't run away."

Denise gave him a wry smile. "I'll try not to."

## Chapter 11

Denise was surprised to get up earlier that morning and find Rhett in her kitchen preparing breakfast. When she'd complimented him on his culinary skills, he countered saying his skill did not extend beyond breakfast. Her cramps weren't as severe as they'd been the day before and she found herself in better spirits.

She'd picked up *The Washington Post* that had been delivered outside her door, and over breakfast they talked then read the newspaper as they'd done as students. Denise was always interested in local politics and world events, while Rhett devoured the business and financial section. He left her apartment to return to his. Instead of leaving her house to arrive at the center at seven, Denise walked in at eight. She'd planned to take Rhett's advice and take more time for herself.

They would return to the Cape the upcoming weekend when Rhett would host an open house coordinated by

Brooke Andersen. It would also be the first time Denise would reunite with his mother since their breakup.

Denise sat at the table in her office with the center's social worker. After the Memorial Day weekend the center shifted to summer mode. The normal Friday-morning staff meetings were staggered with Denise meeting with them individually, because many of the employees, the teachers in particular, had elected to take either Mondays or Fridays off, giving them three-day weekends.

She and Lisa Brown were going over files on the children the therapist had flagged. "What's happening with Angelo?"

Lisa adjusted her half-glasses. Her smooth round brown face belied her age. "He's wetting the bed again, and his teacher noticed a fresh bruise on his thigh. He claims he fell off his bike. The last report of bed-wetting was when his father returned to the house."

"I thought his mother had a restraining order against his father."

"She does," Lisa confirmed.

Denise massaged her forehead, while shaking her head. "Are you certain he's back in the house?"

The retired social worker was a volunteer, working twelve hours a week to offset fees for her two grand-children. Her daughter *and* son-in-law had been deployed to Iraq and Afghanistan, and she'd become temporary guardian for twin toddlers.

"I can't say yes with any amount of certainty."

"Have you talked to Angelo's mother?"

"I tried, but she's too afraid to say anything. Remember, it was her sister who made her call the police when he broke Angelo's arm."

"Call child protective services and have them make an unannounced house call. You also have to let them know about the bruise." The center was mandated by law to report what they suspected to be child abuse. "What else do you have?"

"Miranda says Ms. Vance still hasn't taken DeShawn to get his glasses."

"Tell Ms. Vance that we're going to suspend her son until he gets his glasses. That should get her attention. It's not fair the child has to sit out most activities because he can't see more than three feet in front of his face."

Lisa made notations on a legal pad. "Ms. Clark called me to say she's going to have to pull her son out because her employer has cut her hours and she can't afford to pay our fee."

"Have her bring in her pay stub and we'll adjust the fee. The woman can't keep or look for another job with a child in tow." The single mother had come to the center after her mother, who'd looked after her infant son, passed away.

Lisa smiled, showing off the braces on her teeth. She'd waited until she was in her early fifties to correct an overbite. "That's it, Denise."

Denise smiled. "Thanks, Lisa."

"You're welcome."

She exhaled an audible breath when the social worker walked out, closing the door behind her. Denise didn't think she would ever get used to the number of incidents of neglect and/or abuse when it came to children. A number of New Visions children were in foster care, which was a constant reminder of the breakdown of the family structure. Single mothers, single fathers, divorced parents, grandparents as legal guardians for their grand-

and great-grandchildren, drugs, alcohol, physical and sexual abuse were becoming all too common.

Pushing to her feet, Denise looped the lanyard with her ID around her neck. In addition to her administrative duties, she was the New Visions storyteller. The children loved hearing her read because she was able to change her voice, affecting different dialects and accents, much to their amusement. Today's title for the two- and three-year-olds was Dr. Seuss's *Cat in the Hat*.

Rhett stood over the conference-room table with the Capital Management Properties urban planner and his assistant—an undergraduate student. The constant hammering and drilling coming from the fourth floor was missing. He'd contacted the contractor to arrange for his team to come in after the offices closed for the day. The contractor had reminded him that he would have to charge for the night differential, but it was worth it to Rhett not to be disturbed by the ongoing noise.

Bill Lloyd had spread the architectural plans for the four-square block of commercial property out on the table. "There are thirty-six storefronts—twenty occupied and twelve vacant."

"How many have valid leases?" Rhett asked.

"Fifteen," said the assistant.

Rhett smiled. "That's more than I would've predicted." The former owner had neglected to renew leases, and in the end had stopped making repairs to his properties. "I want you to put a team together to visit each of the merchants and ascertain whether they want to continue doing business. I already have the architect's report as to structural problems in some of the stores. CMP will make the repairs, renovate and update all of the storefronts to give them a uniformed appearance.

Malcolm, I want you to check with the police to uncover which businesses have been targeted for holdups and burglaries. Also, which ones have a heavier than usual number of people hanging out in front of them. Once the area is gentrified the store owners are going to be responsible for enforcing the no-loitering clause in their lease. Teenagers hanging out around corner stores make them easy targets for drug pushers."

Bill Lloyd pointed to the stores highlighted in yellow. "What's up with these?"

Rhett stared at the brilliant urban planner who'd just celebrated his thirtieth birthday. When he'd taken over Capital Management Properties, Bill had elected to stay on rather than look for another position. "One houses a child care center. I've earmarked the adjacent storefront for their proposed expansion."

"That's a prime location because it's corner property," Malcolm said.

"What are you trying to say, Malcolm?" Rhett asked.

He checked the printout listing the rent for the stores. "Isn't the rent rather low for the square footage and location?"

"No."

"No?" Malcolm repeated.

"No," Rhett said emphatically. "New Visions Child-care is a beacon of hope in a neighborhood where parents need a safe place for their children while they work. I will not increase the rent no matter how prime you believe it is."

"But…but you're losing money on the space."

The seconds ticked as Rhett gave the too-eager assistant a lethal stare. "My money, my space."

"Rhett?" Tracy Powell's voice came through the building's paging system.

Walking over to the wall, he picked up the wall phone. "Yes, Tracy?"

"Your mother just returned your call. I have her on hold."

"Please tell her to wait. I'll take it in my office."

Bill placed a hand on Malcolm's shoulder, squeezing it gently after Rhett left the conference room. "A word of caution. Never piss off the person who signs your paycheck."

Preppy-looking Malcolm Robinson gave his mentor a wide-eyed stare. "Rhett didn't seem to be upset."

"Yes, he was. It's just that you don't know him well enough to recognize it. You could have a very bright future with CMP, because we're a young company that's growing when others are struggling to stay afloat. Don't let your mouth get you in trouble."

A beat passed. "Okay," Malcolm said begrudgingly.

Rhett walked into his office and closed the door. He'd called his mother but she hadn't answered the phone, so he'd left a message for her to call him back. Sitting on the corner of the desk, he picked up the receiver.

"Good afternoon, beautiful."

A husky laugh came through the earpiece. "Save that smack for your lady friends."

Rhett smiled. "You don't say that when Maynard calls you beautiful."

Geraldine laughed again. "That's because he's my husband. Now, why did you call me?"

"I wanted to check to see if you're still coming to the

Cape for the week, and also to let you know that I'm bringing a houseguest."

"You don't have to check with me on that, Rhett. After all, it is your house."

"That's true, Mom. Out of respect, I just thought I'd let you know."

"Is there something about your houseguest you aren't telling me?" she asked perceptively.

"I'm back with Denise Eaton."

There came another pregnant pause. "Back how, Garrett?"

Rhett knew his mother was going into serious mode when she called him by his given name. "We're going to get married."

"When?"

"New Year's Eve."

"Have you given her a ring?"

He shook his head, then realized his mother couldn't see him. "No. I'm going to wait for her birthday."

"When is her birthday?"

"It's the end of September."

"Why wait?" Geraldine asked.

"There's no rush, Mom. Denise isn't going anywhere and neither am I."

"If you are truly committed to the woman, then put a ring on her finger. You have no way of knowing who else may be looking at her."

"I'll think about it," Rhett countered stubbornly. He knew Denise much better than his mother did. If he went out and bought her a ring now he knew she would accuse him of trying to manipulate their relationship. She'd committed to a New Year's Eve wedding, and he'd taken her at her word.

"When will you get there?" Geraldine asked.

"We're going up Friday afternoon."

"I have to drop Maynard off at the airport Saturday. As soon I see him off I'll drive up."

"Don't forget I'm throwing a little something and inviting some of my neighbors."

"Have you checked the almanac for the weather?"

Rhett laughed. His mother had more faith in the almanac than the Weather Channel. "What does it say, Mom?"

"There is a slight chance of rain."

"It doesn't matter. We'll just bring everything inside."

"I have to go now. The chef just drove up. Today's lesson is short ribs with leeks and spinach."

"That sounds delicious. Love you, Mom."

"Love you back, son."

Rhett hung up, blowing out his breath. He couldn't understand why his mother wanted him to rush into an official engagement when he and Denise had just picked up the pieces to start over.

Besides, when he bought Denise a ring he wanted her to select the style she wanted, not what he thought she would like. If there was one thing he knew about Denise Eaton, it was that she wasn't shy. If she wanted a ring, then she would make it known. After all, she wasn't reticent when she'd asked him to make love to her.

His private line rang, and Rhett answered the call before it rang again when he saw the name come up on the display. "Thank you for getting back to me. I hope you're calling to let me know you have room for my sextuplets, all who by the way are named Malik."

"Didn't you tell me you have three sons and three daughters, Mr. Fennell?"

"Yes, I did, Ms. Eaton."

"You named your daughters Malik?"

"We call the girls Malika."

Denise's sultry laugh caressed his ear. "You know you're crazy."

"Hell yeah. I'm crazy about you."

"I'm calling to invite you to dinner."

Rhett smiled. "I'll come, but only if we can have a sleepover."

Denise laughed again. "Sure."

"Sure what, Denise?"

"You can sleep over. Don't forget to bring your jammies."

"What time is dinner?" he asked.

"Seven."

"I'll see you at seven."

Rhett was glad that Denise had called, because if she hadn't then he'd planned to call her and invite her to spend the night in his suite at the Hay-Adams. He couldn't wait for the workmen to complete the renovations on the fourth-floor apartment. The space was configured to contain four bedrooms, five baths, a living room and formal dining room and a media room. He'd wanted a full-size state-of-the art kitchen, not the utility ones that came with most apartments. He'd invested a great deal of his personal wealth into renovating two homes, but what good was making money if he didn't take time to enjoy his life?

So many people he'd met hadn't planned for their futures when he was planning not only for his future but also for generations to come behind him. Rhett may not have known his father but what he didn't want was for his mother's bloodline to end with Garrett Fennell.

Pressing a button on the intercom, he buzzed Tracy.

"Please call Mr. Tolpin and see if we can meet at one instead of four. Let him know something very important has come up and if he can't accommodate me, then we can reschedule at his convenience."

He released the button, came around the desk and sat down. Stanley Tolpin was his banker and a financial guru. Stanley had a sixth sense when it came to purchasing or passing on a parcel. Rhett had called Stanley because he'd wanted to discuss the hostile takeover of Chambers Properties, Ltd. He'd forgiven Denise for not trusting him, but Rhett didn't think he would ever forgive Trey Chambers for sleeping with his woman.

# Chapter 12

Denise opened the door, shaking her head when she couldn't make out Rhett's face behind an enormous bouquet of white and pale pink flowers in every variety. "What did you do, buy every flower at the florist?" she teased, smiling.

Leaning over, Rhett kissed her cheek. "Practically. Don't try to carry it," he said when she reached for the vase. "It's too heavy for you."

Resting her hands on her hips, she watched Rhett cross the living room and set the vase on the credenza in the dining area. "How do you expect me to lift it to change the water?"

"You won't have to. I'll come over and change the water."

Denise stared at the exquisite arrangement. "Thank you. The flowers are beautiful."

Rhett slid the strap to a leather backpack off his

shoulder and closed the space between them. Wrapping his arms around her waist, he lifted her effortlessly off her feet. He stared at her scrubbed face, awed that she looked so young even though their birthdays were only months apart. Denise didn't claim the kind of beauty producers wanted for daytime television actresses, but a soft natural beauty that would only improve with age. Wisps had escaped the ponytail, and with her tank top and cutoffs she could easily pass for a high-school coed.

He angled his head, brushing her soft mouth with his. "How was your day?"

Looping her arms around Rhett's neck, Denise buried her face against his strong neck. "It was good." She told him about her storytelling session with the children where she broke character and ended up laughing harder than any of the children. Teachers from other classrooms had come in to see what the hysterics were about.

Rhett lowered her until her sandaled feet touched the floor. "You know you missed your calling."

"What's that?"

"You should've become an actress, because you have a flair for being quite dramatic."

Denise's hands slid down the front of his shirt, under the hem and up his bare chest. "My, my, my," she drawled in a flawless Southern inflection. "Ah had no ide-ah you wah so strong, dah-ling."

Smiling, Rhett caught her hands, stopping her from arousing him further. It would be a few more days before he would be able to make love to her again. The brief encounter had served to whet his voracious appetite for Denise. What he hadn't understood was how Denise had believed he was sleeping with another woman. When he hadn't been in class, working or with his study group they'd been together.

The summer months had been excruciatingly lonely for him. Denise had returned to Philadelphia while he'd stayed in Baltimore. The bank had offered him full-time employment over the summer and he'd taken advantage of the opportunity because he'd wanted to save money. He'd found himself counting down the days to the beginning of the fall semester, unaware that he figuratively had been holding his breath until he'd knocked on the door to her dorm and waited for her to open it. They'd made love around the clock like rabbits before settling into their familiar routine as if time or space hadn't separated them.

"Why didn't you become a drama teacher?"

"If I'd majored in theater and drama, then I never would've met you."

Rhett nodded. "I hadn't thought of that." Bringing her hands to his mouth, he kissed her fingers, then sniffed them. "I smell garlic and peppers."

"You have a good nose. I'm making roasted bell peppers, couscous-stuffed pork chops and a first course of shrimp with a spicy avocado sauce."

"That sounds good."

"Come to the kitchen with me. I have to check on the pork chops."

Rhett sat on a stool at the cooking island, watching Denise as she moved confidently around the kitchen, chopping, stirring, whisking and blending the ingredients for a spicy avocado sauce. The kitchen wasn't large but the way it was designed maximized every square foot. A pantry and a washer/dryer unit were nestled in a corner, while black granite countertops and appliances broke up the white palette of the floor and cabinetry.

"I spoke to my mother today."

Denise stopped arranging jumbo shrimp on a small baking pan lined with oiled aluminum foil. "Did you tell her about us?"

Rhett met her eyes, seeing indecision in the dark orbs. "Yes. I told her we're planning to marry on New Year's Eve."

"She's probably as shocked as my parents that we're seeing each other again."

"If she is, I didn't detect it in her voice," Rhett admitted. He stood up, came around the island, his arms circling Denise's waist. "Everything is going to work out okay, sweetheart. We don't owe anyone an explanation. All I want from our families is their love and support."

Peering over her shoulder, Denise met Rhett's resolute gaze. "We have that, darling." She closed her eyes, moaning softly when he nuzzled her neck. "What are you doing?"

"I'm kissing the cook."

She smiled. "If you kiss the cook before she finishes the meal, then no one is going to eat."

"Do you need me to help you with anything?"

"You can set the table."

"Do you want candles?" Rhett asked.

Denise rested the back of her head against his shoulder. "Yes. There's a supply of tablecloths and liners in the credenza."

"Should I put out wine or water goblets?"

"Both."

Rhett pressed his mouth to Denise's ear before he released her.

Gathering dishes, silver, stemware and napkins, he walked out of the kitchen to the dining area to set the table. He'd stopped, a long time ago, trying to analyze why he'd fallen in love with Denise Eaton and not some other woman. At first he'd believed it was because he'd taken her virginity—that it was out of guilt that he'd continued to see her. It had taken a month, another thirty days, before he'd made love to her again. On the second encounter, his willingness to bring her pleasure while denying his own had been the single most telling act of selflessness. From the very first time he'd slept with a woman Rhett's goal had been achieving an erection, sustaining that erection and ejaculation.

Denise was also different, special, because she was the first woman with whom he'd slept with and hadn't exchanged money for sex. She'd offered him her innocence, love and her heart—precious gifts he'd coveted and treasured.

Never, not even once, had he glanced at another woman when he and Denise were together. And it wasn't as if women hadn't passed him their phone numbers or devised schemes to get him to come to their dorms to study, while others had been bold enough to ask if he would sleep with them.

If he'd been different, if he'd been like some men who didn't have to go looking for sex, he could've slept with a different woman every night of the week. But that hadn't happened because he'd committed to one woman, Denise Eaton.

Stepping back from the table, he surveyed his handiwork. He'd learned to recognize formal and informal table settings when he attended the boarding school, but it was Denise who'd taught him how to set a table. Even when they'd ordered takeout or pizza, he would set the table at his dorm with paper napkins, plates and plastic forks and spoons. It took about two weeks before Denise let it be known that she detested eating off paper plates with plastic utensils when she handed him a shopping bag with plates and flatware and glassware with a four-piece place setting.

Rhett had teased her, calling Denise Miss Prissy, but it had been too late. He'd fallen in love with the girl with the brilliant smile, quick mind, sexy voice, unyielding drive and impeccable manners.

Denise walked into the dining area with a carafe of ice water and another filled with a chilled rosé. "The table looks nice." Going on tiptoe when Rhett took the carafes from her, she kissed his jaw. "I think I'm going to keep you for a long, long time, Garrett Fennell."

"How long is a long time?"

She scrunched up her nose. "I'd say give or take a couple of lifetimes."

"That sounds about right."

Rhett placed the carafes on a handmade oyster-white crocheted tablecloth with a matching liner. He remembered when Denise had bought the tablecloth. They'd driven up to Lancaster, Pennsylvania, when he'd talked about seeing the Dutch Country. He and Denise had spent the weekend touring, eating and shopping. They'd returned to Baltimore with the trunk of her car filled with homemade quilts, candles, tablecloths and jars of jellies and preserves. After he'd moved to Philadelphia to work and attend graduate school, Rhett had found himself drawn back to the epicenter of the Amish country where the appeal of simplicity and community were interchangeable.

"Rhett!"

He blinked as if coming out of a trance. "Yes?"

"You looked as if you just zoned out on me for a minute."

"I was thinking about the time we drove to the Amish country."

Denise's eyelids fluttered wildly when she recalled the weekend that had almost changed her life and their future. It'd been the first and only time they'd made love without using protection. Her menses, which had always come on time, was late and she spent the next two weeks in dread. Rhett, who'd appeared totally unaffected by their dilemma, said that *if* she was pregnant they would marry and he would drop out of college to work and support her. She'd screamed at him, saying she wasn't going to let him forfeit a full academic scholarship because they'd been irresponsible. Fortunately, she wasn't pregnant and after a thorough examination her gynecologist prescribed an oral contraceptive to regulate her cycle.

"Were you thinking of the time when we had unprotected sex?" she asked in a quiet voice.

"No, Denise. I wasn't thinking of that time."

"I'm going back on the pill." She'd called her gynecologist, who'd told her to come into the office. He'd given her several samples to see which brand she could tolerate without too many side effects.

Rhett's eyebrows lifted a fraction. "When will you start?"

"I'll take the first one Thursday. I don't want us to have to deal with an unplanned pregnancy when we have to plan a wedding and honeymoon."

The mention of a honeymoon brought a smile to Rhett's expressionless face. "Where do you want to go on our honeymoon?"

"It has to be someplace warm. There's no way I'm

going to marry on New Year's Eve in the northeast, then hang out at a ski resort."

"You have a choice between the Caribbean, Hawaii or Tahiti."

Denise ran and jumped into his arms, and he swung her around and around until she felt the room spinning uncontrollably. "You know I've always wanted to go to Tahiti," she said breathlessly when he stopped.

"How long do you think you can stay away from your babies?"

"At least two weeks." Even if she hadn't hired an assistant director by December, Denise knew Lisa Brown was more than capable of running the child care center in her absence. The retired social worker had spent her entire career in a school setting.

"Make it three and we'll take side trips to Australia and Hong Kong. I heard shopping in Hong Kong is the bomb."

"I'll see what I can do," she whispered against his firm mouth. Denise kissed him again, pulling his lower lip between her teeth. "Put me down, darling. It's time to eat."

Dinner became a leisurely affair. Denise dimmed the overhead chandelier, and lit a quartet of fat pillars but hadn't drawn the drapes at the window spanning the living and dining area, and the lights in buildings and monuments in the nation's capital provided a romantic backdrop for the two people sitting opposite each other talking quietly as a radio station tuned to soft jazz filled the apartment.

The meal had turned out better than Denise had expected. Roasted shrimp, brushed with hot-pepper sauce and sprinkled with cumin seeds, were placed on lettuce leaves and covered with a spicy sauce made with chunks of avocado, tomato, coarsely chopped white onion and finely chopped jalapeño chiles. She'd added a couple of tablespoons of fresh lime juice and salt, putting all of the ingredients into a food processor to pulse them to form a chunky purée.

She altered the recipe slightly for the couscous-stuffed pork chops when she'd coated them with orange marmalade and dried currants. Denise had gotten the recipe from a parent who sat on the New Visions Childcare board of directors. She'd served warm buttered pita bread and roasted bell peppers to accompany the meat dish.

Rhett patted his flat belly over his shirt. "I think you've got your mother beat in the kitchen, baby."

"Don't even try to play yourself," Denise drawled. "You know my mother can cook rings around me. Even Grandma Eaton had to admit that Paulette Eaton was a better cook than she was, and that was something extraordinary coming from a woman who never took to any of her daughters-in-law. For some reason she thought they weren't good enough for her *boys*."

Rhett smiled at Denise over the rim of his water goblet. "You don't have to worry about not getting along with your mother-in-law. My mother adores you." He set down his glass. "Now that we're on the topic of weddings, do you want to get married in a church or a catering hall?"

"I'd say a catering hall if it wasn't a holiday. Chances are most of them will be reserved for New Year's parties. What if we marry at my parents' house? It's certainly large enough to hold a hundred people comfortably if we remove the furniture from the living and dining rooms."

Rhett nodded. Boaz and Paulette Eaton owned a large

house set on several acres in an exclusive Philly suburb. "Who are you going to get to do the officiating?"

"My father, of course."

"He's going to perform the ceremony *and* give you away?"

"No," Denise said, laughing softly. "Xavier can give me away. Do you plan to have any groomsmen?"

Rhett nodded again. "I'm going to ask my mentor from Marshall Foote Academy to be my best man and my stepfather to be a groomsman."

She thought about Rhett's choice—older men who'd impacted his and his mother's lives. Had his mentor replaced the father he never knew and was he grateful for the man who'd changed his mother's life?

Denise knew if she and Rhett hadn't separated, Trey Chambers would've been his best man. Both had attended the same prestigious boarding school, were college business majors and in a study group together. They'd referred to each other as "brother," were close or even closer than brothers who shared a bloodline.

Trey, who purportedly couldn't be faithful to one woman, had earned the sobriquet Casanova. Denise had been exempt from his charm and advances because she'd been Rhett Fennell's woman. She'd gone to Trey after discovering Rhett's betrayal, staying in his apartment until she'd gathered the strength to return to her dorm. She'd submitted the paper on Statistics and Research Methods and packed up her room, arranging for the contents to be shipped back to Philadelphia. Later that afternoon, she'd gotten into her car and driven home. It had been two days before graduation. Her parents hadn't seen her walk across the stage to receive her degree, and she hadn't been there to watch the man she'd loved receive the highest honor bestowed on the student with a perfect 4.0 GPA.

"Who do you want in your bridal party?"

Rhett's query broke into her musings. "I'll probably ask Chandra to be my matron of honor and Belinda a bridesmaid. If you can come up with one more groomsman I can either ask Zabrina or Mia. I'd probably choose Mia, because she's the only one who won't become a mother this year."

"Speaking of mothers—have you told your mother she's going to be mother of the bride?"

Denise traced the stem of the wineglass with her forefinger. "Not yet. I've decided to tell her in person. Dealing with Mom on the phone is like pulling a wisdom tooth with dental floss."

Rhett chuckled. "She's not that bad, baby."

"You say that because she's not your mother. I love her dearly, but nothing is easy when it comes to Paulette Eaton."

"Do you want me to come with you when you tell her?"

"No. But, thank you for asking." Denise blew him an air kiss. "Are you ready for coffee?"

Rhett, pushing back his chair, stood up. "Don't get up. I'll make it."

Denise waited for Rhett to walk out of the dining area and then got up and began clearing the table. He shot her an angry glare when she entered the kitchen with plates and serving pieces. Things had changed but they hadn't. He'd cautioned her about getting up because Rhett knew she couldn't remain seated. She'd always appreciated his help, but whenever he cleared the table and scraped plates a fork or serving piece would invariably be missing.

"Not to worry about your silver," Rhett drawled facetiously. "I now count the number of place settings, and if one is missing I check the garbage."

"Thank you, baby," she crooned.

He smiled. "You're welcome, baby."

The rain came down sideways and Rhett turned the wipers to the highest setting. The almanac was right when it'd predicted rain for Friday and intermittent showers for Saturday. He'd told his mother the weather wasn't a factor in canceling the soirée because he'd planned for an indoor or outdoor gathering.

He'd conferred with Denise as to the menu for the small crowd of thirteen and then called Brooke Andersen with their preferences. They would offer a cocktail with the requisite crudités and hot and cold hors d'oeuvres on the terrace, weather permitting, or in the living room. An informal sit-down dinner, weather permitting, would be served under a tent on the terrace with a DJ providing musical selections spanning several decades.

The event coordinator had reassured him she assumed the responsibility for ordering flowers, hiring the waitstaff, bartender, DJ and personnel to set up and clean up. All he and Denise had to do was look pretty. Rhett had invited couples he'd met at the few social events he'd attended on the Cape, in addition to his architect, who'd confirmed he would attend with his wife. Tapping a button on the remote device, Rhett maneuvered into the driveway at the same time the automatic garage door opened.

Denise waited in the car as he entered the house to check around. He lingered long enough to adjust the thermostat and then returned to the garage to escort her inside before emptying the trunk of groceries and luggage. He'd suggested she pack enough clothes and personal items to last throughout the summer months; he was stunned into speechlessness when he stored four pieces of luggage in the trunk of his car.

They'd worked quickly, storing perishables in the refrigerator and freezer before filling pantry shelves with staples. She'd unpacked her bags, putting everything away in the walk-in closet, when Rhett joined her. His hair was so close-cropped she could see his scalp.

Crossing his arms over his chest, Rhett angled his head, staring at the feminine curves so blatantly outlined in a pair of hip-hugging jeans. "I came to ask if you would be interested in sharing my hot tub."

Denise gave him a sensual smile, her lips parting to reveal straight white teeth. "What else are you offering besides a hot tub? After all, I do have one in my bathroom."

"What about a personal masseur?"

Denise assumed a similar pose. "And what else?"

"I'm willing to rub lotion all over your body."

"And what else?" Denise crooned, closing the distance between them.

Rhett dropped his arms with her approach. "I'm going to kiss you, starting with your face and ending at your feet." He winked at Denise. "I just might take a slight detour at a rest stop to get something to eat."

Heat flared in Denise's face like opening the door of a blast oven. "Your offer is beginning to sound very tempting."

"What else do I have to do to tempt your further?"

"I want to go to the rodeo."

Bending slightly, Rhett scooped her up into his arms. "Hee-haw!"

# Chapter 13

Rhett walked out of Denise's bedroom and into his. Lowering her feet to the carpet, he took his time removing her clothes: blouse, bra, jeans and bikini panties. His eyes ate her up when his gaze lingered on the slender body with curves that never failed to send his libido into overdrive.

She was slimmer than she'd been years ago, but her breasts, although small, were firm, perky. They were what he thought of as a handful and mouthful. Cradling her face in his hands, he kissed her, teasingly at first before taking full possession of her mouth and increasing the pressure until her lips parted under his sensual assault.

Denise held on to Rhett's wrists as she felt herself being pulled under and down into an abyss of drugging pleasure from which she didn't want to escape. She'd become his and he hers the first time they'd lain together in a sparsely decorated dorm. The room had become their sanctuary where they'd shared secrets and whispered promises. It had been where they'd planned for their future, a future that included marriage and children. They'd pretended they were married, repeating vows to love and forsake all others until death parted them. However, it hadn't been death that had torn them asunder but lies and distrust.

She'd walked around hemorrhaging emotionally. As she'd thrown herself into teaching the bloodletting had subsided and she'd stopped crying herself to sleep. Dating Kevin had become a welcome diversion, because he'd been someone she could talk to other than her family members. Someone who'd filled the empty hours when she hadn't been preparing lesson plans or meeting with parents to discuss their children's progress or lack thereof. He'd been there when she'd needed a date or escort to a social function, and he'd been there when the built-up sexual frustration had become so intense that it had kept her from a restful night's sleep. The single encounter with Kevin had been blatant proof that she hadn't gotten over Rhett Fennell.

Denise had shocked her family and herself when she decided to open a child care center in D.C. She'd almost convinced herself that moving from Philadelphia to D.C. was because research indicated the need for quality child care was greater in that particular D.C. community than in her hometown. It hadn't been until the contents of her co-op were loaded into the moving company's truck that she had been able to admit her decision was predicated on the expectation that she would run into Rhett again. It had taken two years, and now that they were given a second chance at love she would cherish every precious minute of her life with him.

Moaning softly, she undid the buttons on Rhett's shirt, her fingers trembling in her attempt to free the buttons from their fastenings. She managed to get two unbuttoned before Rhett finished the task. Her gaze never left his when he kicked off his running shoes, unsnapped the waistband to his jeans, pushing them and his briefs down and off his hips in one smooth motion and stepping out of them.

Rhett pulled the elastic band from her hair and a riot of curls floated around her face and neck. Her full parted lips, slightly swollen from his rapacious kisses, sensual curls and half-shuttered eyes fired the desire racing headlong throughout his body. He'd had to wait almost a week to make love to Denise again and the respite had tested his patience and resolve not to touch her until she deemed it.

It had taken Herculean strength not to laugh when she'd mentioned rodeo, because it was Denise's favorite position in bed. It had also become a favorite of his because lying on his back while she straddled him prolonged the intense pleasure while delaying his ejaculation.

Wrapping his arms around her waist, he lifted her slightly while walking in the direction of the bathroom. He'd dimmed the recessed lights and opened the French doors, but had left the doors leading out the terrace closed because of the driving rain. Music flowed from concealed speakers. Rhett stepped into the hot tub, and gently lowered Denise until her feet touched the bottom. He sat down, easing her gently down as the warm soothing waters bubbled up around her breasts.

Resting her head on Rhett's shoulder, Denise closed her eyes. "I can't think of a more perfect way to unwind at the end of a workweek."

Burying his face in her hair, Rhett emitted a guttural groan. "Ditto. We can come here every weekend if you want."

"I want," she said, sounding like the children at the center. For the two-year-olds it was "no," and the three- and four-year-olds it was "I want."

Rhett nuzzled her ear. "I told you before if it's within my power then I will make it happen."

"What if it's not within your power?" she asked.

He chuckled deep in his throat. "Then, I'll pay someone to make it happen."

Denise wanted to ask Rhett if that was what he'd done—if he'd paid someone to uncover that she'd leased the space before he bought the land on which the child care center sat, but knew it would open the proverbial can of worms and that was something she wanted to avoid at all costs.

In the past they'd rarely argued, but when they had it was as if they'd unleashed all the hounds in hell. They had gone to their respective dorms and waited for the other to apologize. Three days had become the limit, and when they'd reunited the makeup sex had been explosive.

She gasped when his hands covered her breasts, thumbs moving back and forth over the nipples until they were hard as pebbles. One hand moved down her belly to her thighs. She gasped again when he touched the sensitive nodule at the apex of her vagina.

Denise moved her hips against his hands, the warm water serving to increase the rising heat between her thighs. A long shudder shook her when he inserted a finger between the wet folds, her pulsing flesh opening and closing around his finger.

Rhett hardened quickly and he withdrew his hand,

turning Denise around to face him. Holding his erection in one hand, he guided it between her legs, both sighing in unison when in that instant they became one with the other.

Reaching down, he grasped her knees and her legs went around his waist. Being inside Denise without the thin barrier of latex made him harder, his fingers gripping her hips as they slammed into each other. It wasn't lovemaking but mating as the sound of heavy breathing drowned out the soft strains of light music.

Denise held on to the rim of the teak tub, her hips moving against the hardness sliding in and out of her body like a piston. A guttural moan escaped her parted lips when she bared her throat. Rhett had taken her breast into his mouth, his teeth nipping at the distended nipple until she mewled like a wounded creature. One of the side effects of the oral contraceptive was tender breasts, and the pain-pleasure had her close to fainting.

The slight flutters she'd tried to ignore grew stronger and stronger and she tried thinking of any and everything except the delicious sensation of her lover's hard sex pushing in and out of her vagina.

The muscles in Rhett's neck bulged as he tried holding back. "Let it go, baby."

"No!"

"Please, oh please," he pleaded. If he didn't come he was afraid his heart would explode.

Denise let go of the edge of the tub, her arms going around Rhett's neck. She buried her face against the side of his neck, her breath coming in hiccupping gasps. "Oh, oh, oh!" The litany escalated, echoing in her head like a needle stuck in the groove of a vinyl recording.

Rhett pulled out and stepped out of the tub without releasing Denise. Walking on bare feet, while dripping water on the teak floor, he made his way out of the spa, through the bathroom and into the bedroom. He fell across the bed, bringing Denise down to straddle his thighs.

They shared a knowing smile when Denise sank lower and lower until Rhett was fully sheathed between her thighs. Their passion revived, she rode him fast and hard, he bucking like a rodeo horse.

Rhett's heat and hardness responded to the newly awakened sensuality that had lain dormant for years. As her passion rose higher and higher so did his until it exploded in an awesome, vibrating liquid that scorched her mind and her body, leaving her limp, sobbing and convulsing in an ebbing ecstasy.

The rush of his release left Rhett light-headed. Somehow he found the strength to reverse their position, breathing heavily to force air into his lungs. There was only the sound of their labored breathing in the stillness of the bedroom as they lay motionless, reliving the aftermath of a sweet fulfillment making them one with the other.

"Hee-haw!" Denise whispered in his ear.

"Ditto, baby. Dit-to!"

The rain had stopped and pinpoints of light pierced the watery sky as the sun rose higher. Denise, leaning against the door frame, watched Rhett help his mother as she stepped out of her car. It'd been a long time since she'd last seen Geraldine Fennell, but time had seemingly stood still for the tall, slender woman who'd passed her features along to her only child. At forty-six, she looked at least ten years younger. A smile touched her mouth as Geraldine touched Rhett's cheek, Denise finding the gesture loving, gentle.

The glow of loving and being loved had lingered long after she'd forced herself to leave the bed where she and Rhett had spent most of the night making love. He'd kept his promise to give her a massage, followed by slathering her supple body with a scented cream. She'd fallen asleep under his sensual ministration, and when she'd woken hours later she'd returned the favor; it had been her mouth and not her hands that had left Rhett pleading for mercy. The impasse had ended when he'd managed to free himself from her rapacious mouth to ride her until spent.

Denise's smile grew wider. The delicate circle of diamonds on Geraldine's hand sparkled. Her future mother-in-law was now a married woman.

Geraldine Russell glanced around Rhett's shoulder, her gaze meeting and fusing with the young woman who'd enthralled her son in a way no other had before or after her. Denise Eaton had changed. It wasn't the longer hair, but something else, something that wasn't discernible at first glance.

When she approached Denise, who'd straightened from her leaning pose, she saw determination in the dark eyes that didn't waver. She hadn't only matured, she'd grown up. She extended her arms, and she wasn't disappointed when Denise moved into her embrace.

"Welcome back—daughter."

Denise hugged Geraldine tightly, kissing her soft cheek. "It's good to be back—Mother."

Easing back, Geraldine smiled at the girl she'd always wanted as her daughter-in-law. "He loves you so much, Denise," she whispered.

Denise's gaze shifted to Rhett, who was unloading the trunk of his mother's car, then back to the older woman with chemically straightened hair, parted off-center chin-length blunt-cut ends. "He loves me and I love him." A beat passed. "This time we're going to get it right."

"We'll talk later," Geraldine whispered as if they were coconspirators.

The rains had stopped completely, the sun had dried up the moisture soaking the earth and the afternoon temperatures were climbing steadily to the low eighties. Brooke Andersen arrived at the house at three and minutes before a pickup truck bearing the logo of the florist emblazoned on the side doors parked behind her white Escalade. The caterer, waitstaff and DJ weren't expected to arrive for another two hours. The printed invitations had read: cocktails at 6:00, dinner at 7:30 and fun until ???

Denise and Geraldine walked a short distance from the house to keep out of the way of the workers who'd come to erect the tent and set up tables and chairs. Rhett had remained behind to oversee the setting up. The two women sat on a stone bench flanked by large stone planters overflowing with a profusion of sweet pea and peonies. Leaning back on her hands, Denise stared at the calm surface of the water. There was a comfortable silence until Geraldine exhaled a sigh.

"When Garrett asked me to come with him to see this property I thought my son had taken leave of his senses. The house was large, but falling apart. And there were so many weeds I was afraid to walk anywhere because I didn't know what I would step on. He was so excited about buying a house that I didn't have the heart to tell him he was throwing away his money. I was wrong and he was right—as usual."

Denise leaned forward. "As usual?"

Geraldine turned to stare at Denise staring back at her. "When you and Garrett broke up…" Her words trailed off. "When you left my son," she continued, "I was afraid Garrett was going to hurt himself."

Denise felt her heart sink like a stone in her chest. "You…you're not talking about suicide?" Much to her surprise, Geraldine laughed.

"No, Denise. Garrett loves life much too much to take his own. I'm talking about physical pain. He'd become an insomniac. If he wasn't working he was studying. And when he could find the time, he was seeing women—a lot of women."

Denise felt as if someone had put their hand around her throat, squeezing and cutting off oxygen to her lungs. Rhett hadn't mourned their breakup, but had replaced her with what probably had been a long line of nameless, faceless women.

"Everything came to a head when he had a problem with one of his supervisors," Geraldine continued. "What he hadn't realized at the time was it was a blessing in disguise. He left Philly, moving back to D.C., where he stayed with me for about three months. During this time he spent countless hours in the library and on the Internet learning everything he could about the real estate market. After he purchased a foreclosed house, he secured a loan to rehab it and eventually sold it for a three hundred percent profit. It was, like the kids say, on and poppin'. He claimed buying and selling real estate was like crack cocaine. It was that addictive."

She sighed again, this one louder and longer. "I'm going to tell you about Garrett's father. It's something I've never told anyone—not even Garrett, and I want you to swear you won't tell him."

Shaking her head, Denise closed her eyes for

several seconds. "I can't do that, Mother. I've been given a second chance with Rhett and I'm not going to jeopardize our future together by keeping secrets. If you don't intend to tell Rhett, then please don't tell me."

Geraldine crossed her outstretched legs at the ankles, staring at her toes painted a flattering raspberry shade pushed into a pair of leather thongs. She'd carried the secret for almost thirty years, and she wanted to unburden herself. A wry smile parted her lips. "I can see why my son fell in love with you, Denise."

"Why's that?"

"You're loyal, caring and selfless."

Denise placed an arm around Geraldine's slender waist. "I love Rhett. I think I fell in love with him at first sight. We've had our ups and downs like most couples, and even when we were apart I never stopped loving him. If you love Rhett as much as I know you do, then give him some peace. Please tell him about his father."

Resting her head on the younger woman's shoulder, Geraldine nodded. "I know I'm going to have to do it."

"Please do it before we officially announce our engagement on my birthday." Denise and Rhett had discussed a timeline for their engagement and wedding, deciding three months was long enough for an engagement for a couple who'd met for the first time ten years ago.

"That doesn't give me much time, but I suppose I'll work up enough nerve before then. Maybe I should give him a special birthday present when I reveal who his daddy is." Her son would celebrate his twenty-ninth birthday August fifteenth. "I'd offered to come and stand in as Garrett's hostess before I realized you were going to do it," Geraldine said, deftly changing the topic of conversation.

"You can still do it," Denise teased, laughing.

"Nope. If I'm going to do any hosting, then it's going to be for me and Maynard. As soon as my husband returns from his conference, I want you and Garrett to come for a visit. I'm taking cooking lessons, so I promise not to treat you guys as guinea pigs."

"What have you learned to cook?"

The two women spent the next forty-five minutes talking about food. Denise revealed the number of meals that had ended in disaster before she'd been able to complete one that was palatable. It had taken her a while to come to the conclusion that she would never surpass Paulette Eaton's culinary expertise, who'd been taught by her mother, and was resigned that she'd become a competent but not a fabulous cook. She was a lot more creative when it came to planning a menu for entertaining. She'd planned the menu Brooke had passed along to the caterer.

Denise had become the consummate hostess, standing alongside Rhett as they greeted their guests with handshakes and welcoming smiles. A black and white silk faille striped, sleeveless dress, nipped at the waist and ending at her knees and a pair of black patent-leather Louboutin slingback stilettos complemented Rhett's black linen Hermès suit and white shirt he'd elected to wear outside the waistband of his slacks. He'd also foregone a tie for the evening. She tamed her curly hair with a gel, while brushing it until she was able to pin it into a loose twist behind her left ear.

Brooke Andersen flitted around like an anxious stage mother waiting for her child to be auditioned, making certain the waitstaff saw to the needs of Rhett's guests. Her husband ignored her antics as he and a group of men discussed their golf handicaps.

"You look beautiful, Mother," Denise whispered to Geraldine. A light coat of makeup highlighted her attractive features. A narrow headband made from peacock feathers held her hair off her face, while a black silk man-tailored blouse, white silk slacks and black ballet-type slippers flattered her tall, slender frame.

Geraldine flashed a demure smile. "Thank you, Denise. If I'd harbored any doubts about the woman who Garrett would end up with, they were dashed tonight when I saw you with my son at what will be the first of many gatherings the two of you will preside over."

A slight frown found its way between her eyes before Denise replaced it with a slow smile. Geraldine had said *preside over* as if she and Rhett were heads of state. Was that, she mused, how she'd thought of her son? Was he the issue of some prominent black Washingtonian?

What she couldn't understand was why Geraldine was so willing to divulge Rhett's father's identity to her and not to him. Of course she wanted to know who'd fathered the man she planned to marry, but not if he didn't know.

Her eyes lit up when she spied Rhett's approach. He was carrying a flute with a sparkling liquid; she recalled the bottle of champagne he'd ordered the night they'd reunited at The Lafayette.

Rhett handed Denise the flute, his eyes roving appreciably over her body before coming to rest on her face. He found her perfect from head to toe. The four-inch heels were sexy and showed off her curvy calves and slender ankles to their best advantage.

"I had the bartender fix that for you."

Hoisting the flute, Denise saw a dollop of dark syrup in the bottom. "What is it?"

"It's called a kir royale. It's made with crème de cassis and champagne. The cassis is made from black currants," he explained when seeing her puzzled expression.

She took a sip, holding the liquid in her mouth for several seconds before letting it slide down the back of her throat. "This is good." The cassis was a sweet contrast to the dry champagne. She took another sip. "I think I've finally found a cocktail I like."

Rhett leaned in closer to her. "Don't let the fruity drink sneak up on you."

Denise brushed a light kiss over his mouth. "I'm not driving, so I figure I can have a couple of these babies." She kissed him again. "Will you save me a dance, darling?"

Rhett angled his head, smiling. Seeing Denise totally relaxed, smiling and outgoing filled him with a pride he hadn't known existed. She'd become the perfect hostess and assuredly a perfect wife and mother. Even Brooke had complimented him on Denise's menu choices. She'd selected buckwheat blinis with sour cream and caviar, spicy shrimp crostini, fresh salmon tartare croutes and spicy pork empanadas with a chunky avocado relish. Asian-inspired hors d'oeuvres included fresh herb and shrimp rice paper rolls with peanut hoisin dipping sauce, sushi rice, wonton wrappers with herbed prawn and a tangy lime dipping sauce and salmon caviar sushi rice balls.

A carving station with rib roast, turkey breast and grilled plank salmon, along with grilled vegetables and salad greens, had been set up for buffet-style dining. The dessert menu included tiny chocolate cups filled with white chocolate mousse, mango and mascarpone cream, kiwi raspberry and lime mousse and sweet tartlets with fillings ranging from cherry and almond, citrus ginger cream and summer berries.

Entertaining on the terrace under the tent created a fairy-tale atmosphere with baskets of colorful flowers. The view of the Chesapeake in the foreground was awe-inspiring. Japanese lanterns, suspended from the poles holding up the tent, would be lit at sunset.

"I'll save more than one dance," he whispered in her ear.

Denise found it odd that she and Rhett were the youngest couple in attendance, most of the others ranging from their mid-thirties to fifties and possibly sixties. Again, when he mentioned those he wanted as groomsmen in their wedding party the men were older than him. She didn't know his D.C. social circle, but she was willing to bet they, too, were older than Rhett by at least a decade. And it wasn't for the first time that she wondered if he connected with older men because he was looking for a father figure.

Couples had set down their drinks and tiny plates with hot and cold appetizers to dance to the monster Black Eyed Peas hit "I Gotta a Feeling." Denise and Rhett exchanged smiles and winks, then joined the others. The DJ alternated upbeat tunes with slower ones, allowing those wishing to dance a respite to eat and drink. It was only when everyone sat down to eat that the music changed to softer relaxing instrumentals.

It was close to midnight when guests reluctantly took their leave, thanking Rhett and Denise for their generous hospitality, while reminding them to keep their weekends open during the summer so they could return the favor.

Geraldine had retired to her first-floor bedroom,

pleading fatigue because she'd gotten up hours before dawn to drive her husband to the airport two hours before his scheduled flight.

Denise, standing barefoot in the bathroom slathering cream on her face before she removed it with a damp cloth, saw Rhett's reflection in the mirror over the vanity. "It was a wonderful party."

He came closer. Droplets of water shimmered on his wide shoulders from his shower. "You were wonderful."

Lowering her head, she splashed water on her face, nearly choking when she felt his erection pressing against her hips. "Can't you wait for me to wash my face and take a shower?" she asked, patting her face dry.

"You don't need a shower, baby."

"No, Rhett!" Her protest came too late when he picked her up, carrying her back into the bedroom.

Everything became a blur when Rhett made love to her with an intensity that stole the breath from her lungs. His tongue journeyed down her body, tasting every inch of flesh while branding her as his. She opened her arms and her legs when he moved up over her, welcoming him inside her. Denise struggled, but was unable to hold back the moans of erotic pleasure that became screams of ecstasy when she stiffened with the explosive rush of orgasmic fulfillment. The screams faded to surrendering whimpers of physical satiation as she closed her eyes and reveled in the rush of Rhett's release bathing her still-throbbing flesh.

They lay together, limbs entwined until Rhett pulled out, rolled over and gathered her against his body. Minutes later they slept the sleep of sated lovers.

## Chapter 14

"Mom, will you please stop crying."

Paulette, dabbing the corners of her eyes with a tissue, narrowed them. "Are you getting married because you're pregnant?"

Denise threw up her hands. "No, you didn't say that," she whispered not to be overheard by those at a nearby table at her mother's favorite D.C. restaurant.

She'd called her mother to let her know she was driving up to Philly to see Belinda and Griffin's infant son, but Paulette had informed her she and a few of her sorority sisters were going to New York to attend a Broadway show and take in the sights. She'd promised to come to Washington to visit with her before returning to Philadelphia.

Sitting up straight in a huff, Paulette squared her shoulders. "Well, are you?"

"No, Mother. I am not pregnant." Denise had

punctuated each word. "I'm not getting married until December. If I were pregnant, I wouldn't wait that long."

Eyelids fluttering wildly, Paulette smiled brightly. She pressed her palms together. "I hope you're going to ask your father to do the officiating."

Reaching in her handbag, Denise removed an envelope, pushing it across the table. "I've written down some things I'd like to incorporate into the ceremony and reception. Rhett and I will officially announce our engagement on my birthday and will exchange vows New Year's Eve. Because most catering halls will probably be booked for the holiday, I thought having it at the house would be the perfect venue to combine a wedding while welcoming in a new year."

Paulette rested her hands over her heart. "Thank you, my darling. You don't know how happy it makes me to hear you say that. Your father keeps complaining that the house is too big for two people, that he wants to downsize and moved into a townhouse like Dwight and Roberta. But I'm constantly reminding him that we're the only Eatons in Philly with a house large enough to accommodate the family whenever they get together. Now that Belinda and Griffin have a new baby I doubt if they're going to be doing that much entertaining. By the way, did you get to see the baby?"

Denise nodded, smiling. "I did. Oh, Mom. He's adorable."

"He looks just like Griffin."

"I agree," Denise said. The baby boy, who'd been named Grant in honor of Griffin's late brother, was all Rice. It appeared as if the only thing Belinda had done was carry the boy to term. When she'd asked Belinda if she was going back to teaching in September, the history instructor still hadn't decided whether she wanted to stay home and raise her son and nieces or hire a nanny to care for the baby. Although Griffin worked from home there were occasions when he had to go out of town on business.

"All I can say is that in another twenty years he's going to break a lot of hearts. Now, when are you going to shop for wedding gowns?"

Denise didn't think she would ever get used to her mother jumping from one subject to another without taking a pause. It was as if her brain functioned faster than her mouth.

She indicated the envelope, which Paulette hadn't bothered to open. "It's all in that envelope. But to answer your question, I'll probably start looking in November. I'm not going to deal with countless alterations and fittings if I gain and lose weight over several months."

Paulette surveyed her daughter with a critical eye. "You are a little on the thin side."

"Remember, I always gain weight during the winter." She closed her eyes, smiling. "I have grits at least once a week from November to late March. Come April 1, I swear off grits and the weight comes off."

Paulette was saved from asking any more questions when the waiter arrived with their dining selections. She glanced at her watch. "I have three hours before my train leaves." She'd taken the train from Philly to New York, then from New York to D.C.

"Don't worry, Mom. I'll make certain you get to Union Station on time."

Denise didn't tell her mother that she had to go home and prepare for a fundraising event for later that evening. Although she would sit on the dais with other board members, she'd asked Rhett to accompany her.

\* \* \*

Rhett got out of the car, handing the keyless device to the valet. He reached for the jacket to his tuxedo, slipping his arms into the sleeves, and then came around to assist Denise. When he'd arrived at her apartment to pick her up he'd found himself unable to speak. Her obligatory little black dress was exactly that—little. Strapless with an empire waist and ending several inches above her knees, it displayed an inordinate expanse of velvety brown skin. Matching silk-covered stilettos with ties wrapping around her ankles directed attention to her smooth bare legs and groomed feet.

Resting a hand at the small of her back, he pressed his mouth to her ear. "If any man looks at you sideways I'm going to kick his ass," he said, smiling.

Denise stiffened before relaxing against his splayed fingers. "What's this all about?"

"Your dress, or the lack of it, *baby*."

"There's nothing wrong with my dress, Rhett."

"So you say," he mumbled. A swell of breasts rose and fell with each breath.

They walked into the mansion where the organization dedicated to raising funds for college scholarships for disadvantaged high-school students had contracted to hold their annual dinner dance.

"Denise."

She turned when she heard her name, smiling at one of the volunteers. "Yes?"

"They want all of the board members seated on the dais *now*."

Denise rested a hand on Rhett's lapel. "I'll see you later, baby. I told them to put you at a table close enough to the dais so I can flirt with you during the boring speeches."

Rhett resisted the urge to laugh when Denise turned her heels and sashayed, her hips swaying sensually in the revealing dress and high heels.


"When did you and Garrett Fennell hook up again?"

Teeth clenched, Denise leaned to her left. Whoever had arranged the seating had sat her next to Trey Chambers. Good-looking, smooth-talking Trey had been blessed with the charm of a pimp seducing women into his lair and the morals of an alley cat.

"That is none of your business."

"What I don't want to believe is how you can take up with him again, knowing he can't be faithful."

"Again, that's none of your business. Now, if you don't take your hand off my shoulder, I'm going to hurt you."

Trey dropped his hand. "What's the matter, Denise? Are you afraid your boyfriend is going to say something?" His voice was so low the woman sitting on his left couldn't overhear what he was saying. "It's funny he never said anything when he came to my apartment and I told him we were sleeping together."

She went completely still, unable to move even if her very life depended upon it. "What did you say?"

Trey's eyes filled with contempt. For years he'd stood in Garrett Fennell's shadow. There weren't many black students at Marshall Foote Academy and for some unknown reason the instructors had always compared his grades to Garrett's, and he'd come up short. Very, very short. He'd had to study around the clock and bust his ass while Garrett had earned As without opening a book.

It had been the same at Johns Hopkins, but things had changed when he and Garrett joined the same study group. Garrett had become his unofficial tutor, helping him when they had studied for exams and editing his papers. He'd hated Garrett as a boy and even more so as a man. He hated his confidence, smug attitude *and* his brilliance.

"After you found that naked girl in your goody-two-shoes boyfriend's bed, you came running to me because I was your precious Rhett's best friend. You kept asking me why he would sleep with her when he had you, and I told you some men are dogs like that. But you neglected to ask me the most important question, Denise."

"I asked what I needed to ask," she spat out. "And that was how you could hit on your best friend's girlfriend when you knew what I'd been through."

"Remember, Denise, you'd broken up with Garrett *and* because you were no longer sleeping with Garrett, I saw you as fair game."

She rolled her eyes. "To you, any skirt is fair game."

"Whatever works," Trey drawled. "What I couldn't believe was your naiveté. When I started the rumor that Garrett was sleeping around you swallowed it hook, line *and* sinker." He stroked the nape of her neck. "You never asked how that hooker got into Garrett's room," he crooned. Denise slapped at his hand, but he tightened his grip on the back of her neck. "I made a copy of his key and gave it to her. What made the ruse so easy was you were so damned predictable. I knew you always went to Garrett's dorm on Wednesdays, because his last class ended at six. So, when you walked in on Bubbles she gave you an award-winning performance."

Twin emotions of rage and relief surged through Denise as she tried to process what Trey had just revealed. She'd wanted to tell him he was lying, but couldn't. He'd set her up. He'd also set up Rhett. But why?

Grabbing her forehead, she counted to ten in an attempt to control her rising temper. She reached for her evening bag. "Don't ever come near me or speak to me as long as you live." Denise pushed herself in a standing position, and on trembling legs managed to make her way off the raised stage without falling. She didn't see Trey wink at Garrett sitting at a table a short distance from the dais when he, too, stood to follow her.

Rhett, who had crossed his arms over his chest, lowered them. He'd sat silently, watching the man who at one time had been as close to him as a brother. But that all had changed when Trey told him that Denise had come to him distraught because she'd found a naked woman in his bed, and in her grief she'd asked him to make love to her and he had.

Trey had been one of the Marshall Foote students who'd gone with him on what they'd called their "panty raids." There had been times when Trey had given him money to buy sex when he'd run short on funds. They'd become brothers in every sense of the word, swearing an oath never to hit on the other's woman. It was easy for him to keep his promise, because once he'd begun sleeping with Denise Eaton he'd never looked at another woman.

Pushing back his chair, he wove his way through the tables set in the ballroom, stepping out into an expansive area where formally dressed couples were filing into the mansion. "Did you see where Denise Eaton went?"

he asked the woman sitting at a table checking tickets against a computer printout.

She pointed to a door to her left. "She's in there."

Taking long strides, he reached the door and turned the knob. It opened and what he saw made his blood run cold. Trey, who'd grabbed the area between his legs, was on the carpet writhing in pain. "You bitch!" he hissed between his teeth. Tears were streaming down his face.

Denise stood over him, one hand curled into a tight fist. "I told you not to touch me!"

Rhett kicked the door shut, closing the distance between him and his childhood friend. He rested his foot on Trey's neck. "If I ever hear you call her a bitch again I will kill you."

Trey shuddered violently. "She kicked me in the balls."

Leaning over, Rhett increased the pressure on the hapless man's throat. "She had a good reason for kicking you in the *balls*. I'm only going to warn you this one time—stay away from my fiancée." He removed his foot, his eyes dancing wildly when he looked at Denise. "Let's go!" Cupping her elbow, he led her out of the room. "Miss Eaton isn't feeling well, so I'm taking her home," he informed the woman at the table.

"Rhett, please slow down," Denise pleaded when he forcibly pulled her along with him.

He gave her a warning stare. "Please, don't say anything to me until we're out of here."

"Slow down now!" He shortened his strides, permitting Denise to keep up with him.

The valet seemed shocked when Rhett told him to bring his car around. He gave the young man a generous tip and peeled out of the parking lot on two wheels after he and Denise were seated and belted in.

"I don't know what kind of game you're playing, Denise, but it has to stop. You let some man feel you up, then when you decide you've had enough you kick him in his groin. Do you realize I was a minute away from crushing his windpipe?"

"For your information I didn't let him feel me up. I'd warned him if he didn't take his hands off me what I'd do."

"Why didn't you just get up and change your seat?"

"I needed to hear the truth, Rhett."

"What are you talking about?"

Denise told him everything. "What I can't understand is why he'd felt the need to break us up."

Rhett's hadn't realized he'd had a death grip on the steering wheel until he felt the tingling in his fingers, indicating he'd impeded blood flow. Never had he wanted to hurt someone as he did Trey Chambers. He'd lived for twenty-eight years without having or wanting to fight, or defend himself using his fists, but that had all changed within the time it took for Denise to relate what she'd been told.

He placed his right hand on Denise's knee. "It's okay, baby. I'll take care of Trey Chambers." What he didn't tell her was that what he'd planned for Trey would devastate him more than a beating.

"No, Rhett. I don't want you to take care of him."

"What *do* you want?"

"I want you to leave him alone. He can't hurt us any longer."

Rhett chuckled despite the seriousness of the situation. "I think you hurt him enough." He gave Denise a quick glance. "Damn, girl. You should register those stilettos as a lethal weapon."

Denise sucked her teeth loudly. "He's lucky I didn't stomp on his package."

"Ouch! Remind me never to piss you off."

She smiled, covering the hand resting on her knee. "You don't have to worry about that. I would like to have your babies."

Rhett blew out a breath. "I guess that means I'm safe."

"You're safe as long as you don't mess up, Garrett Mason Fennell."

Rhett sobered. "I'm sorry you're missing your fund-raiser, because I don't trust myself not to go back and finish what you started. I promise to send a generous donation in your name."

"Rather than send a donation, why don't you establish a Garrett M. Fennell college scholarship? You're one of D.C.'s success stories, and whether you want to acknowledge it or not, you are a role model."

"You know how I feel about that, Denise. Parents should be role models for their children, not strangers or athletes."

"You're preaching to the choir," she said in a quiet voice. Geraldine said she'd wait until Rhett's birthday to disclose his father's identity, and Denise hoped she'd keep her promise.

Rhett turned down the street leading to Denise's apartment building. "I know we talked about announcing our engagement on your birthday, but I've changed my mind. What do you say we go shopping for rings tomorrow?"

His query surprised Denise, because they'd agreed

to a short engagement period. "What made you change your mind?"

"It was something my mother said about commitment. She told me if I was truly committed to you, then I should put a ring on your finger."

"Ring or not, Rhett, I've always been committed to you."

When he'd heard Denise was staying with Trey, Rhett thought she'd gone to him for emotional support. However, when Trey had opened the door wearing nothing more than a pair of briefs, proudly informing him that he'd been a fool to give Denise up because she was a freak in bed, Rhett had felt as if he'd been stabbed in the gut. Three days. It had taken only three days for her to go from his bed to the bed of his so-called best friend.

"I know that now. Can you forgive me for not staying and fighting for you?"

Denise moved as close to Rhett as the seat belt would allow her. "I forgave you a long time ago. I had to or I wouldn't have been able to get on with my life."

"Unfortunately, it has taken longer for me to get past the need for revenge." He'd forgiven Denise, but didn't believe he would ever forgive Trey. Rhett gave Denise a quick glance. "Even though you're dressed for a night of seduction, I'd like to make a quick detour."

"What are you doing?" She gasped when he unexpectedly executed a U-turn, the squeal of tires leaving skid marks on the roadway.

"I want to take you to see something."

It was another twenty minutes before Denise realized what Rhett wanted her to see. He pulled up in front of a four-story town house blocks from Dupont Circle. A brass plate affixed to the front of the building identified it as housing the offices of Capital Management Properties, Ltd.

Rhett disarmed the security system, escorted her into the building and through a modern lobby with gleaming marble floors. He punched the button for the elevator for the fourth floor.

Leaning against the opposite wall in the elevator, Denise saw a glint of amusement in Rhett's dark eyes. "You've done well, Garrett Fennell."

He winked at her. "And I'll do even better once we're married."

"That's going to happen," she said confidently.

"I know it will." The doors opened on the fourth floor and Rhett stepped out, holding the door for Denise to follow. The tall windows were covered with butcher paper, while naked bulbs hung from the exposed ceilings. He beckoned to her. "Come, baby, and see what will be *our* home."

Denise was confused. "Home?"

He took her hand, leading her around a ladder, sawhorses and other workmen tools. "The offices of CMP occupy the first three floors. This floor will be configured for personal living space. Let me show you the floor plan."

Denise stared at the large architectural rending of what would become a four-bedroom, five-bath residence with a state-of-the-art modern kitchen, home office/ library, theater and exercise room. She pointed to the master bedroom. "I like that we'll have his and her bathrooms." Hers would have a bidet and Rhett's a urinal. "It looks...wonderful."

Rhett heard the hesitation in Denise's voice. "You don't like it?"

"What's not to like, Rhett?"

Reaching for her shoulders, he pulled her to his chest. "Why do I feel that you're not on board with this? Would you prefer living somewhere else? Perhaps in northern Virginia or in one of the D.C. suburbs?"

Denise cradled his face between her hands. "Forgive me, darling, if I look as if I'm not excited about living here. Nothing could be further from the truth. I love this neighborhood. In fact, I'd tried renting an apartment in a town house around the corner, but it was too pricey for my budget." She leaned closer, brushing a tender kiss over his firm mouth. "We're going to have a wonderful life together. It's large enough to entertain and have an occasional houseguest. And when daddy Fennell decides to work late he doesn't have to concern himself with getting stuck in D.C. rush-hour traffic. All he has to do is come upstairs, have dinner with his family and then go back to the office."

Rhett stared at Denise under lowered lids. "We can wait a couple of years before we start filling up the bedrooms with children. I know it would make your mother happy if we started right away, but I'm going to leave that decision up to you."

She scrunched up her nose. "Let's wait a year. If I decide to change my mind, then it'll be sooner rather than later."

He lowered his head and kissed her with all of the passion he could summon at that moment. Trey's revelation had opened the door to their past, but served to put to rest all of the doubts that had plagued him for years. Denise hadn't slept with Trey and she knew he had been faithful to her.

The twisted cretin may have gotten by with his subterfuge for six years, but he wasn't going to get away unscathed. Rhett would make certain of that.

# Chapter 15

Denise sat on her bed, legs crossed in a yoga position, with the cordless phone anchored between her chin and shoulder. "I don't care about your belly. I want you in my wedding party."

"I'm going to look like a beach ball in a gown," Chandra argued softly.

"What am I going to do, Chandra? Zabrina probably will have delivered just before Christmas, so she'll be recuperating. The only one I can count on is Belinda. I still have to call Mia to see if she'll be available—providing she doesn't get pregnant, too."

"Mia's not even dating anyone, so I doubt if she's going to get pregnant. You definitely can count on Belinda and Mia. Zabrina is questionable, and my due date is January twenty-eighth, give or take a week. If I go into labor and spoil your wedding Aunt Paulette will never speak to me again."

"Don't worry about my mother. I'll handle her. And even if you do go into labor, there will be enough doctors in attendance to deliver your baby."

"Bite your tongue, Denise Amaris Eaton. I will not have my father delivering my baby."

Denise laughed softly. "Let's hope you don't have to eat your words. But seriously, Chandra, I want you to be my matron of honor. I haven't begun looking at gowns, but I'll probably choose one with an empire waistline, so your gown will be similar to mine. We can have a Jane Austen–inspired wedding."

Chandra's laugh came through the earpiece. "I don't think you'd want me to expose my chest. I told Preston that for the first time in my life I'm willing to do a centerfold layout. My *girls* are off the hook!"

"What did he say?"

"It's something I can't repeat on an open phone line. But I told him to enjoy them before my belly takes over."

"Are you big?"

"No. I'm getting thick in the waist, but so far no belly." She sighed heavily. "All right, I'll be your matron of honor."

Denise closed her eyes, whispering a prayer of gratitude. "Thank you, cuz."

"You're welcome, cuz. I'm honored you asked me. Now tell me, what does your ring look like?"

Denise held out her hand and described the exquisite diamond engagement ring featuring a cushion halo with a round cut center stone, three rows of micro pavé diamonds on the shank and surrounding the center stone.

"When are you coming to Philly so I can see it?"

"Tomorrow. I have to come up for the closing on the

co-op. If you're not busy maybe you can meet me for dinner."

"Call me when you're finished and I'll come and pick you up."

"Why don't you and Preston come down here a weekend? We can hang out at the house on Cape St. Claire in Maryland."

"I'd love to, Necie, but Preston's still working the final edits for *Death's Kiss*. He's planning a short theatrical production before filming begins—"

"It's going to be a movie?" Denise interrupted.

"Yes. Griffin just negotiated a movie deal with a major Hollywood studio. Griffin insisted on complete literary control on behalf of his client, or he was going to take it to an independent studio. He gave them twelve hours to come back with a yes or no. It took only three hours for them to agree. Literary control has been something Preston has wanted for years."

"You know my father calls Griffin a legal hustler."

"Whatever works," Chandra drawled. "His hustling got my husband what he wants, and when my baby is happy I'm happy."

"I ain't mad at you, cuz," Denise drawled.

"Thank you, Necie. As soon as P.J. Tucker comes up for air we're going to take you and Rhett up on your invitation to come down and hang out with you guys. I overheard Mom talking to Aunt Paulette about not putting on a family reunion this year because Belinda's still recuperating from sixteen hours of hard labor and Myles says the doctor doesn't want Zabrina to travel long distances."

"That's okay. I'm taking some time off in the fall to look for a gown, and during that time I'm going to make my rounds and visit with everyone."

"Is your gorgeous fiancé coming with you?"

"I don't know. Right now he's fixated on some deal that has him getting up out of bed to talk on the phone in the middle of the night. I'm so exhausted that I told him to stay at his place until whatever he's working on is resolved. Unfortunately, I don't do well on three hours of sleep."

"Right now I sleep through everything," Chandra admitted, "and that includes thunderstorms. Don't forget to call me tomorrow."

"I won't. I'm coming up on the train, so maybe we can eat somewhere near the station. My treat."

"You treated the last time. I'm…"

Denise hung up, cutting off what she knew would become a rant from Chandra. Once she deposited the check from the sale of the apartment into the bank, not only would she have more disposable income but she would also amp up her anemic savings account. Unlike her fiancé, who'd paid as much for her engagement ring than she planned to pay for a new car, she had become more discerning when it came to her finances.

Leaning over, she placed the receiver in its cradle when it rang. She picked it up without looking at the display. "Hello."

"What's this I hear about my favorite sister getting married?"

Denise frowned. "Why do you always refer to me as your favorite sister? Does Daddy have a secret love child hidden away somewhere?"

Xavier's smooth baritone laugh came through the earpiece. "Dad may be a badass on the bench, but I know he's not so bad that he would risk cheating on our mother, who probably would make his life a living hell."

A smile replaced her frown. "Mom is worse than

a dog with a bone when she becomes fixated on something."

"I hear you. She's going to love playing the role of mother of the bride."

"I've decided to let her have her wish and go along with whatever she has planned. The only thing I'm going to do is show up and exchange vows with my new husband. I'm certain Mom told you that Daddy is going to do the officiating, so I want you to give me away."

There came a beat of silence. "Are you certain that's what you want, Denise?"

"Of course it's what I want, Xavier. Who else is going to give me away? Besides, everyone in Philly knows Paulette Eaton is the consummate hostess and puts together some of the best parties in the city. That's why she's on all of the social registers of every bougie African-American couple and organization."

"You know how I feel about her fake friends."

"You just don't like them, Xavier, because they're always trying to set you up with their daughters."

"I've never had a problem finding my own women."

Xavier was telling Denise something she already knew. All of her friends in high school and college had wanted her to introduce them to her brother. What most hadn't known was that he had a jealous mistress—the military. Denise didn't know what it was about putting on a uniform, standing in formation and marching for miles with more than sixty pounds of equipment on his back that her brother found rewarding. He claimed it turned boys into men, girls into women, while building character.

"I'd always thought you would get married before me."

Xavier laughed again. "I'm glad you're marrying

Garrett, because now the pressure is off me to give Mom a grandchild."

"Give me time to enjoy being married before I start pushing out grandchildren. Right now there's an Eaton population explosion with Belinda, Zabrina and Chandra."

"True. But all the babies are Aunt Roberta's grandchildren."

"I'm still not going to bow to pressure and have a baby because our mother wants to be a grandmother. Now, tell me, dear brother, are you going to give me away?"

"Of course I will. I'm going to hang up now because the truck with my bedroom furniture just pulled up."

"How's the new house?"

"It's nice. I'll call you later in the week. Love you, baby sister."

"Love you back, big brother."

Unfolding her legs, Denise slid off the bed and walked over to the closet to select an outfit for the next day. Closing on the co-op had been a long time coming, and once the title was transferred to the new owners that phase of her life would be behind her.

Her next move would be from her current apartment to the fourth floor of the town house near Dupont Circle. The contractor projected completing renovating the space by early fall. Then there was the task of decorating the apartment. She knew it would take time to select what she wanted in each room, then she and Rhett would have to wait for the pieces to be delivered. Denise didn't expect to have every room decorated for quite some time, but Rhett had asked her to decide on the furniture for the master bedroom suite so he could move out of the hotel.

She'd tried imagining, and failed, getting up in the morning to go to work where she only had to ride the elevator one floor or take one flight of stairs to her office. Rhett would never have the excuse that he couldn't get to work because of bad weather or traffic jams. She also couldn't complain about him bringing his work home, because his home and his office were in the same building.

Rhett pumped his fist in the air in triumph. Chambers Properties had pulled out of the bidding on the commercial property near Baltimore Harbor, resulting with CMP coming in with the lowest bid. His prospectus included building several middle-income rental units and a nearby shopping center with stores ranging from supermarkets, boutiques and a sporting goods shop to a movie theater with two screens.

"I heard Trey and his father are looking for investors."

Rhett hadn't known what to expect when he'd returned his financial planner's telephone call, but it was not the news that CMP had the winning bid to a parcel of land he'd had his eye on for years. "How much are they looking for, Stanley? Is it doable?" he asked after hearing the figure.

"Hold on, Rhett, let's crunch a few numbers."

The rapid tapping of keys came through the intercom as Rhett waited for the financial guru to work his magic. "If I'm going to take over Chambers Properties, then I want total control."

"You read my mind, brother," Stanley said, chuckling. "I can make it happen if you're willing to sell off your latest acquisition."

"Not happening," Rhett countered. "My fiancée has her day care center on that parcel."

There was another tapping of keys. "What about putting your house in Maryland up for collateral against a short-term, no-interest loan?"

"Make it happen like yesterday."

"Give me thirty-six hours to get the loan approved. Meanwhile I'll contact Chambers and let him know that I represent an anonymous party willing to invest in their company."

"I want to ink this deal before the end of the week." He and Denise were scheduled to spend the weekend with his mother and stepfather.

"Hang up, Rhett, and I'll call Chambers."

Punching a button on the intercom, Rhett disconnected the call. He pushed back his chair and paced the width of his office. For some reason he was too wound up to sit and wait for Stanley's call. In fact, he'd waited long enough to exact revenge on the man whom he'd trusted like a brother, a man whose deceit had kept him from the only woman he'd ever loved.

He and Trey had been, as people would put it, thicker than thieves. Their friendship had begun in boarding school and continued throughout college. Although Trey had inherited his father's good looks and charm, he had always struggled academically. Rhett lost track of the number of papers he'd rewritten for his friend, or the countless hours he'd tutored him for an exam. He'd told Trey he was blessed to have a position waiting for him at Chambers Properties. What he hadn't told Trey was he doubted whether he would've been able to hold down a position outside of his family's business because he preferred socializing to studying.

Being academically inept hadn't stopped the indulgent

only child from concocting a scheme that would've worked if Rhett hadn't been so in love with Denise. Even after he'd blackmailed her into dating him again, he realized he'd never stopped loving her.

He had promised Denise he wouldn't hurt Trey. He knew she was talking about physically hurting him, when his intent was to cause psychological pain—namely humiliation. The man had to pay for stealing six years of his life.

His private line rang and, taking long strides, Rhett picked up the receiver before it rang again. "Yes?"

"We're on for Friday morning. I told Trey Jr. that I would meet with him, his father and the board at ten o'clock. We'll discuss the terms of the takeover, take a vote, then sign the necessary documents. I also told Trey, without mentioning your name, that you had a prior engagement and will join everyone at the luncheon following the board meeting. The only thing I'm going to tell you is that I don't want to be anywhere close to that restaurant when the fireworks begin."

Rhett smiled. "Don't worry, friend. There won't be any fireworks." And there wouldn't be. It wasn't his style. He'd executed one other hostile takeover, resulting in little or no casualties, and he was certain it would be the same with Chambers Properties, Ltd.

Denise walked out of the bathroom, a towel wrapped around her head, turban-style. Rhett had decided to change their sleeping venue and had spent the past two nights at his suite in the Hay-Adams. It was very different not to have to make the bed, clean up the bathroom or cook. His suite was on the top floor, which offered unobstructed views of the White House.

Rhett was in bed, talking quietly into the tiny

microphone attached to his cell phone earpiece. The television was tuned to a station featuring a local D.C. news program. She crawled into bed with him, supporting her back against a mound of pillows on the king-size bed. She liked the suite because the French doors opened onto a small balcony.

Dinner had become a romantic affair when they'd ordered room service. She'd lit candles while Rhett found an all-music radio station featuring classical selections. They'd shared entrées of goat cheese and basil ravioli with spicy black olives, tomato sauce, capers, pine nuts and shaved parmesan and sautéed sole with parsley potatoes and lemon caper sauce.

Swinging her legs over the side of the bed, she walked over to the thermostat, adjusting the temperature. Although the space was icy-cold, it didn't seem to affect Rhett, who had left his chest bare after pulling on a pair of cotton lounging pants. He lifted his eyebrows questioningly when she met his gaze, pantomiming rubbing her bare arms. Nodding, he returned his focus to his phone conversation.

Denise knew she had to compromise, or her marriage to Rhett wouldn't survive its first year. He was a businessman, and that meant he would spend hours in meetings, on the phone or computer. Rhett had promised not to conduct business at home after eleven at night. The exception would come when they moved into the town house where he would have access to his office 24/7.

Rhett managed to concentrate on what Stanley was telling him even though he'd found his mind straying. Denise had emerged from the bathroom in a revealing black lace midriff top with a matching pair of bikini panties. She came back to the bed, moving closer and resting a bare leg over his.

Everything was in place. The meeting for his takeover of Chambers where he would hold the controlling share of the decades-old real estate corporation had been confirmed. Stanley would negotiate on behalf of a CMP holding company, which made it virtually impossible for Chambers to identify the players. But then even if he knew that Garrett Fennell was his mysterious investor he doubted if Trey could afford to turn away monies needed to keep his company afloat. The next step was filing for bankruptcy and financial ruin for the family and the company's shareholders.

He reached for the television remote, increasing the volume when a special bulletin flashed across the screen. "Stan, let me call you back." Rhett ended the call, staring at the large flat screen. He heard what the newscaster was saying even when he didn't want to believe it. Someone had assaulted Trey Chambers Jr. and left him for dead. When his father was notified of the attack, he'd collapsed and was transported to the same hospital where his son was undergoing emergency surgery.

"You didn't!"

Rhett's gaze swung from the screen to Denise. Her eyes were large and filled with unshed tears. "What are you talking about?"

Denise slipped out of bed as if in a trance, backing up when Rhett reached for her. "Don't touch me!" She hadn't realized she was screaming. "You promised me you wouldn't hurt him."

Ignoring her protest, Rhett pulled her up close in a punishing grip. "How many times do I have to prove myself to you, Denise? When I told you I wouldn't hurt Trey Chambers I meant it."

"Why is he in a hospital fighting for his life, Rhett?"

"I don't know, baby. It's not because of anything I've said or done. Do I dislike Trey Chambers? Yes. But not enough to have someone beat him and dump his body in an alley. There are other ways of making him pay for his sins without resorting to violence."

Denise went completely still. "How?"

"That doesn't concern you," Rhett countered.

"What do you mean it doesn't concern me? Are we going to start keeping secrets from each other even before we're married?"

"Whatever goes on with CMP is *my* business, Denise, and I don't intend to involve you in it."

"How dare you…" The hotel phone shrilled loudly, preempting whatever Denise was going to say.

Rhett released Denise and reached for the receiver. "Fennell," he said, identifying himself. "Calm down, Mom. I can't understand a thing you're saying if you don't stop crying. Okay, I'm coming." He slammed the receiver in the cradle. "Get dressed. My mother wants to see us."

"Now?"

"Yes now." Rhett had slipped out of the lounging pants and was searching through a drawer for his underwear by the time Denise was galvanized into action. It took five minutes for her to slip into a pair of underwear, jeans, T-shirt and running shoes. Damp curls hung around her face, and she managed to grab her handbag before Rhett took her hand as they raced out of the suite.

## Chapter 16

Only the slip-slap of tires on the roadway shattered the silence inside the car as Rhett exceeded the speed limit during the drive from D.C. to Falls Church, Virginia. He could not have imagined what had happened to trigger his mother's histrionics. The sign indicating the number of miles to Falls Church's city limits came into view.

Denise bit down on her lip, wishing Rhett would ease his grip on her left hand. He drove with his left, while holding her fingers captive in his right. It was as if holding on to her would keep his anxiety at bay.

She'd tried imagining why Geraldine had called, asking to see not only Rhett but her, but was unable to come up with a plausible reason. What Denise did not want to entertain was the possibility that something had happened to her husband. Geraldine and Maynard had recently celebrated their first wedding anniversary and… Her thoughts drifted off, dissipating like a puff of smoke. She closed her eyes and when she opened them again Rhett had turned down a winding path to a cul-de-sac with a sprawling Shingle Style bungalow set back from an expansive manicured lawn. He maneuvered into the circular driveway to a home ablaze with light.

Denise always waited for Rhett to get out and come around to open the door for her, but tonight was different. She was out of the car before he cut off the engine. The front door opened and Geraldine stood in the doorway, waiting. The car's doors closing sounded unusually loud in the stillness of the warm summer night. The hoot of an owl and the incessant chirping of crickets serenaded the quiet countryside.

She waited for Rhett, and hand-in-hand they approached Geraldine Russell. Her hair, held off her face with a wide headband, looked as if she'd combed it with her fingers. The T-shirt she'd put on backward over a pair of cropped jeans was evidence she'd gotten dressed in a hurry, or in the dark.

Geraldine kissed her son and the young woman she'd come to think of as her daughter. "Thank you for coming so quickly." Even though she had Maynard, she'd felt as alone and frightened as she had at sixteen. She opened the door wider. "Please come in." Denise walked into an entryway, Rhett following, and she closed the door behind them.

"Where's Russ?" Rhett asked, looking around for his stepfather.

"He won't be joining us."

"What's going on, Mom? You called me in hysterics asking me and Denise to drop everything and come here, and now you tell me your husband won't be joining us. Did he do something to you?"

Geraldine rested a hand on her son's shoulder. "No. Maynard Russell would never hurt me."

"Where is he, Mom?"

"He's in the bedroom. I told him that it would go better if I was alone with you and Denise to tell you—"

"You're not sick?" Rhett asked, as fear filled his eyes.

A hint of a smile broke through Geraldine's expression of uncertainty. "No, I'm not sick. Come in the kitchen. I just brewed a pot of coffee."

Denise lagged behind, staring in awe at the living room filled with light from diamond-paned windows or light screens. Antique runners on gleaming wood floors imbued a sense of warmth and richness, and artificial light diffused through colored panels and skylights were reminiscent of the style attributed to Frank Lloyd Wright.

The smell of freshly brewed coffee lingered in the kitchen as Rhett wrapped an arm around Denise's waist and led her over to a breakfast nook, seating her on a cushioned bench seat at the rectangular oak table.

"Sit down, Mom. I'll bring the coffee."

He poured coffee into delicate china cups for his mother, Denise and himself, placing them on the table already set with place mats and serving pieces. The silence in the room was deafening when he opened the refrigerator for a container of cream. He sat down beside Denise and opposite Geraldine, watching her under lowered lids as she added dollops of cream to her coffee until she achieved the shade she sought.

"We're ready." It was his signal for her to talk.

Geraldine stared at her cup. Overhead light glinted off the older woman's flawless dark face. "What I'm about to tell you should've been told years ago." Her head popped up, her gaze steady. "I've lost count of the number of times you've asked me about your father, and I never could work up the nerve to tell you, Garrett, until now."

His hands tightened around the china cup. "Why did you change your mind?"

Picking up a napkin, she blotted the corners of her eyes. "I don't want him to die without giving you a chance to meet him."

Rhett leaned forward. "Is *my* father dying?"

"I don't know. The last news report was that he'd suffered a massive heart attack." Her reply was a whisper.

Suddenly it hit him, the realization rocking him to the core. "Is Trey Chambers Sr. my father?" Geraldine nodded as tears streamed down her face unchecked. Rhett got up and sat next to her. Reaching for a napkin, he wiped gently at her tears. "Tell me about it, Momma."

Geraldine broke down, sobbing inconsolably. Her son calling her Momma was like going back to a time when she fought to keep her son safe, to make sacrifices in her life so he wouldn't repeat her life and that of his grandmother's.

"I was sixteen when I met Trey for the first time," she said after she'd regained control of her emotions.

Rhett and Denise listened, stunned as Geraldine told of working part-time at a restaurant to earn money to help out her single mother and save enough to pay for her senior prom. She had put off plans to attend college part-time because her mother's asthma had made it more and more difficult for her to work.

Trey would come to the restaurant several nights a

week and sit at Geraldine's table. "He was the foreman at a construction site in my neighborhood, but what I hadn't known at the time was his father and uncles were in the business of buying up properties in low-income D.C. and Baltimore neighborhoods. Some they renovated but many were left to deteriorate. He would leave me tips that the other waitresses would have to work a week to collect.

"First there was the money, then gifts like gold earrings, a silk scarf, a shopping spree where I would select beautiful lingerie and cashmere sweaters. When I asked him why he was spending so much money on me he said it was his wish to make me happy. Of course, he being older said all the things I wanted to hear. What I hadn't known at the time was he was dating another woman in his social circle. I'd become the plaything across the tracks that kept him occupied when his fiancée was busy with her Jack and Jill and sorority meetings.

"Everything came to a crashing halt when he told me that he had to get married to save his father's company. In other words, it was to be a marriage of convenience. What I hadn't known at the time was that his girlfriend was pregnant and they'd opted to marry sooner rather than later that year. The day I discovered I was also pregnant was the day my mother died from an asthma attack. The social worker from social services arranged for me to live with my aunt, who'd never married or had children. She asked me once who the father of my child was. I was too ashamed to tell her, and she never asked again. I dropped out of school and went to work while Aunt Audrey watched my son."

Rhett closed his eyes, digesting what his mother had revealed. "Why," he asked, opening his eyes, "did you enroll me in Marshall Foote knowing your former lover's son was also there?"

Geraldine's eyes narrowed. "It was the only way I could make him pay for his deceit. I knew he would send his son to the boarding school, because he'd been one of four students who'd integrated Marshall Foote back in the day. I wanted him to see that I'd moved on, and that he'd given me a gift that was priceless. When he saw me with a young boy whom he knew had to be his son I thought he was going to pass out. I could see him mentally doing the math, and I told him Garrett was *my* son, would never be his and I had no intention of messing up his so-called perfect life."

"What did he say, Mom?"

"Thank you."

Rhett blinked. "That's it?"

Geraldine gave him a tender smile. "That was it. I read later that his wife had filed for divorce and Trey was already looking for her replacement. It was apparent Trey could not remain faithful to any woman."

"Like father like junior," Rhett mumbled under his breath. "Do you know if senior told junior that we were half-brothers?"

"I don't know. That's something you're going to have to ask him when…or if he survives."

Rhett, still numbed by the news that he and Trey Chambers were brothers, placed his hand over his mother's. "Have you told Russ?"

Geraldine grew teary again. "Yes. I had to tell him."

"What did he say?"

"What he always says. He loves me." Blowing out her cheeks, Geraldine stood up. "Let me go and get my husband. It's time I introduce him to his future daughter-in-law."

Denise waited for Geraldine to walk out of the kitchen, then moved to sit beside Rhett. He took her hand, threading their fingers together. She didn't say anything only because she didn't know what to say, knowing it would take time for Rhett to come to grips with the revelation that his brother had systematically planned to destroy his happiness.

She rose to her feet when Maynard Russell entered the kitchen, walking into his outstretched arms. Russ was only several inches taller than his wife. His light brown skin was still smooth; dimples and a sprinkling of freckles afforded him a boyish look. His graying sandy-colored hair was cropped close to his well-shaped head.

"We finally meet," Maynard said, kissing her cheek. "Gerri has been bragging about her beautiful daughter and I agree with her. You are lovely."

Denise nodded, pressing a light kiss to his jaw. "Thank you, Father."

Maynard glared at Rhett over her shoulder. "You call me Russ, while this beautiful child calls me Father. Son, you've picked a real winner."

Crossing his arms over his chest, Rhett winked at his mother's husband. "What can I say? We've got impeccable taste when it comes to women."

"No lie," Maynard drawled. "You guys must be exhausted, so I want you to bed down in one of the guest rooms. Everything will look clearer in the morning."

"Come, darlings," Geraldine crooned, leading the way out of the kitchen. Rhett and Denise exchanged a glance, then followed.

\* \* \*

Trey Chambers Sr. survived his heart attack and sailed down to his vacation home in San Juan, Puerto Rico, to convalesce. It took Trey Jr. longer to recuperate. The assault had left him with a concussion, six broken ribs, a broken nose, fractured leg and cheek.

Rhett found himself spending hours in his brother's hospital room, waiting for him to surface from his heavily drugged state so he could ask questions and put their past to rest. He had Stanley Tolpin contact the board members of Chambers Properties to inform him that his client was still interested in investing in the real estate company. Instead of a takeover, his client now sought a partnership.

"Mr. Fennell, Mr. Chambers is lucid and can speak to you now."

Rhett popped from the chair like a jack-in-the-box. He'd spent the past hour in the hospital's solarium, reading. He smiled at the nurse. "Thank you."

He hadn't realized how fast his heart was beating until he walked into the private room to find Trey sitting up in bed. Most of the bruises dotting his face were beginning to fade. A two-week stay in a hospital room had robbed his olive complexion of its natural rich color.

Standing at the foot of the bed, he and Trey engaged in a stare-down. "How are you feeling?"

Trey ran a hand over his hair. "I've been better." He closed his eyes. "Just say better than the other day."

"What happened?"

"I got my ass kicked."

Rhett's impassive expression didn't change. "Why?"

"I owe gambling debts."

"How much do you owe, Trey?"

"A lot."

"How much is a lot, *brother?*"

Trey closed his eyes. "You know?"

"Hell yeah, I know. What I want to know is when did *you* know?"

Trey's chest rose and fell heavily. "When Dad found out that you were graduating at the top of the class and I was near the bottom he let it slip that the son of a high-school dropout was smarter than one whose mother had graduated college with honors. That's when he told me you were his son. I'd always been jealous of how easy it was for you to get As, when I was lucky to get a C. Then, when you'd managed to snag one of the prettiest, most intelligent black girls on campus I knew I had to mess up your perfect world."

Rounding the bed, Rhett sat on the chair next to the bed. "It looks as if your perfect world has imploded. I'm not going to pay off your debts. I'm willing to make Chambers Properties a partner of CMP. *Your* father will be given a generous retirement package, while you will be demoted. I will pair you up with someone who knows the ins and outs of the real estate business. You will be evaluated at the end of a year and, based on your job performance, I'll decide whether to keep you on or fire your ass."

"What about my debts? The moment I walk out of this hospital someone will be out there waiting for me."

"I don't want to know who you owe. However, I'm going to send someone to see you and you'll give him the name. Then, he'll negotiate with your loan shark as to how he wants to be paid. The first thing you're going to put on the table as a bargaining chip is your Thoroughbred."

"No!"

"Yes, Trey," Rhett countered heatedly. "It's betting on something with four legs that put you in that bed, and if you don't want to end up in a box six feet under, then you will sell the horse. My person will have you sign a power of attorney, giving him the authority to sell the animal to pay off your debts. Tell me now if you agree with what I'm proposing, because when I walk out of this room the deal will be off the table."

Trey nodded. "Okay."

Rhett leaned over, patting his shoulder. "Hurry up and get well, brother. You're going to have to work for the first time in your worthless life."

He walked out of the room and bumped into Denise. She'd called to tell him she would meet him in the hospital's visitor parking lot. "I know I'm early, but I didn't want to wait downstairs."

Rhett angled his head and took possession of her sweet mouth. "Let's go to the Cape."

Denise rested a hand over his heart. "You want to go tonight?"

He gave her a tender smile. "Yes, tonight. It's been too long since we've had a quiet evening at home."

"How long has it been, darling?" Denise asked.

"Too long, baby."

And it had been. Since Geraldine's frantic telephone call it was as if their cloistered world had been turned upside down. He'd spent most of his free time at the hospital, and when he went home to Denise it was to fall asleep in her scented embrace.

He loved her, loved her more than he could've imagined loving a woman.

He'd waited six years for her. But now he was counting down the months, weeks and days when he would claim her as his wife. Denise Eaton had tempted him not once, but twice, and both times he'd succumbed to the woman who'd captured his heart forever.

\* \* \* \* \*

# REQUEST YOUR FREE BOOKS!

## 2 FREE NOVELS
## PLUS 2 **FREE GIFTS!**

KIMANI™ ROMANCE

### Love's ultimate destination!